Tainted

Broken Boys, Volume 4

Zane Menzy

Published by Zane Menzy, 2023.

This is a work of fiction. Similarities to real people, places, or events are entirely coincidental.

TAINTED

First edition. October 23, 2023.

ISBN: 979-8223150282

Written by Zane Menzy.

Chapter 1

THE CARAVAN WAS YELLOW on the outside and an even brighter shade of canary on the inside, but I suppose it beat living on the streets. According to the chatty campground manager, who'd been surprised to hear who I was looking for, Damian had upgraded from a shared cabin to his own caravan just a few days ago. I could only assume that Damian had used some of my money he stole to upgrade.

Reclining on the narrow bed at the rear of the caravan, a shirtless Damian sat with his legs spread and his crotch framed by red, baggy satin boxer shorts. The fact it was early afternoon and my former babysitter still hadn't bothered to put pants on spoke volumes about his motivation levels, and employment status.

He may have only moved into this yellow shack on wheels seven days ago but he'd already made it look lived in. Clothes and shoes were scattered all over the threadbare carpet, and the tiny kitchen also looked to be in a similar state of disarray. If it were up to me then there would be no way I'd be visiting Damian in this yellow shitpit. The only reason I had come here was because Jockey had told me to.

1

"I didn't expect to see you when I opened the door," Damian mumbled as he lit himself a cigarette. "Thought you'd still be pissy at me about last night."

"I was in the area so I thought I'd drop by."

The paper at the end of Damian's cigarette crackled as he sucked a deep draught of smoke into his lungs. Staring at a stain in the carpet, he let the smoke back out.

"So do you have any plans for the rest of the day?" I asked.

"Nup."

"Not going out anywhere?"

"Nup."

I tried not to look at the hair on his legs, hairs that disappeared inside the red boxers towards a cock that I was now all too familiar with.

"What's the real reason you're here?" Damian asked abruptly, ending what had been a lingering awkward silence. "And don't give me some bull teko answer. Just be straight up."

"The reason I'm here is to see if you'd like to come with me to get a test. An STD test."

"Say what?"

"An STD test. The health clinic is open until four on Saturdays and I thought maybe we could go together. For moral support."

"You have got to be fucking kidding me." He exhaled a sheet of smoke and eyed me through its whorls. "You actually think I gave you diseases?"

"I just thought it would be safe to check."

"If you're that fucking worried then go on your own." He rest his cigarette down in an ashtray beside the bed. "I ain't pissed razor blades in over a year, bro."

"That's not as reassuring to hear as you think it is."

Damian chewed on a thumbnail for a few seconds before placing his hands on his knees. "I guess not," he muttered. That same thumb he'd had wrapped around his lips a second earlier absentmindedly reached inside his boxers to give his nuts a scratch. "I'll come with you if you pay for it."

"It's free to get tested."

"In that case I'll come with you if you pay me."

"You can't be serious?"

"Do I look like I'm joking?"

"Fine. But I've only got twenty dollars on me."

"*And* you gotta let me take a shower at your place on the way back."

"You do realise there are showers here, right? I walked past the ablution block on my way here."

He gave me a smile, one that wasn't entirely nice. "But they're coin-operated."

"Then cash in the twenty dollars I'm going to give you."

"But that'll be a ball-ache. Easier if you just let me use yours." He sat there watching me with a half grin, half leer. "Besides, the only reason I need a shower so badly is because you left me with a bad case of shit-dick."

"I did not!"

"Come sniff my dick if you don't believe me."

"Fine," I huffed. "You can have a shower at my place."

"While we're on the subject of last night," he said, "you took a damn good dicking, young Michael. You must be feeling it today. Probably a bit sore, yeah?"

"Not at all," I said, and smiled, feeling the beginning of triumph stirring within me. "Your cock isn't big enough to do any damage."

"You ain't exactly hung like a porn star yaself, snow ho."

While it felt good to know I'd just pissed him off, I knew I'd have to forfeit what felt like a small victory. "Sorry. I didn't mean to be rude."

"The fuck you didn't."

I took a quick breath, willing myself to say what Jockey had told me to. Words that according to my master that I would be saying a lot over the next twelve months: "The truth is it was an honour to be fucked by you. To be fucked by a real man."

"Come again?"

"It was an honour to be fucked by you."

The words came out like chunks of vomit; hard, painful and burning.

Snickering, he cocked one leg up, bringing his heel in next to his buttock. The change in posture opened the leg hole of his boxers right up, giving me an eyeful of hairy ballbag. "Whatever you've been smoking, bro, you need to give me some."

"I haven't been smoking anything."

"If you're not high then you must be a fucking idiot. You shouldn't be feeling honoured, you should be feeling ashamed. I made you a Hickford Homo last night. Ain't nothing honourable about that."

Hickford Homo. Hickford Homo. Hickford Homo.

The words knocked about in my brain, leaving me dizzy.

"And you know what that means, don't you?" Damian glared. "If anyone finds out you'll be a fucking joke around this town."

"I know."

"And you're proud of that?"

My spine straightened, my shoulders squared up, but I forced a cool smile onto my lips. "I'm proud that it was a real man who did it to me."

4

"Why are you talking like this?"

"Like what?"

"Like a crazy person."

You knew shit was bad if Damian Takarangi, one of life's greater fuck-ups, called you crazy.

"I'm not crazy," I said.

"Are you sure about that?" He glanced at the floor, but when he met my gaze again, his eyes held a low fire. "You know I only fucked you last night to get back at you, right?"

"I sort of gathered that."

"So you agree you deserved it?"

I told him what he wanted to hear. "Yes. I deserved it."

Swallowing my pride still wasn't something that came naturally to me, but I was learning fast. It might have helped in this particular instance if Damian spun my wheels, but he didn't really. Don't get me wrong, he was okay. Certainly fuckable. But his average looks—and below average hygiene—wasn't the stuff of wet dreams.

My left ass cheek suddenly vibrated, and a whistling noise emerged from my phone. I snatched it out of my pocket and pressed the button to illuminate the screen. It was a text from Jockey.

Jockey: Have you taken the whore to get tested yet?

The text irked me. But there wasn't much I could do about that. I was the one who had fucked up by letting Damian bareback me, and as a result Jockey had decided to push the start date of our contract out for another week. It was only then that I had realised that while I feared being under his control I also craved it, and I had been genuinely disappointed to learn I would not have access

5

to the scruffy stoner's cock until he had confirmation Damian was disease free.

Another text came through. A photo. Jockey lying on his bed, one arm behind his head, his torso stretched out, his skinny boy abs giving way to the brown fuzz of his pubic hair, and just the very top of his cock above the lower frame.

Seeing that Damian was busying himself with another scratch of his balls, I flicked Jockey a response that showed just how desperate and horny I was for his body.

Mike: You are so hot Sir!!!

Jockey: LOL I know bitch. If u bring the whore here after you've been to the clinic then I'll reward u with a mouthful of cum.

Mike: Why do you want to see Damian?

Jockey: So we can have ourselves a friendly chat.

That sounded ominous. The thought of Jockey having a chat with Damian filled me with dread, but not enough to put me off wanting to swallow Jockey's tasty load. Without responding, I pressed the button that turned the screen dark and then put my phone back in my pocket.

It was time to spoon-feed Damian some bullshit.

"Gavin just text to say he's got his girlfriend over and asked me to stay out of the house for a while so they can have some privacy."

Damian giggle-snorted. "Is he getting frisky is he?"

"It sounds a lot like it. Which means you won't be able to have a shower there."

"What the fuck? That's not on. You promised."

"It's okay. We can swing by my friend Jockey's place after we've gone to the clinic. He won't mind letting you use his shower."

"Jockey?" Damian's tongue licked out, moistened his lower lip, and then disappeared. "Is that the crazy honky who wears all that army shit?"

"That's the one."

"That dude's a fucking nutter, bro."

"Do you know him?"

"Not really. But I know his brother. We shared a cell together for a while when I went away." I was about to ask which brother he was referring to—both of Jockey's older brothers had done stints in jail—but Damian soon clarified. "Darren was alright. We got on pretty good."

"Did Darren ever ask you to drop the soap while you were cell buddies?" It was a shit joke but I couldn't resist.

Damian glowered. "You shouldn't joke about that sort of thing. That sort of thing really does go down in there."

As if I hadn't put my foot in it enough already, I said, "Sorry. Were you, uh... you know?"

That earned me a vehement shake of the head. "Fuck no. No bastard laid a hand on me in there. Those niggers prefer their prison wives to look like you...*and Darren.*"

Conspiracy lurked behind his bitter sneer, and his stormy eyes glimmered with secrets. They locked onto mine; for a nanosecond we were mentally connected and information had been exchanged.

I wonder if Jockey knows? was my first thought. If he found out the big brother he idolised so much had been raped in prison it would be akin to telling a four year old that Father Christmas isn't real.

"So," I said abruptly, keen to change the topic. "Shall we get going?"

"Give me a minute to wake up a bit more. I only got out of bed when you knocked on the door." As if to emphasise his point, Damian let out a roar-like yawn, stretching his arms above his head.

I looked at his armpits, the black hair tangled in there. My dick reacted positively to the sight, even though I'm sure his pits must have been rank.

I'm not sure why but I'd been fascinated by men's armpits ever since I was a kid. Somewhere along the way though that fascination turned into a sexual interest. I think it may have been because during puberty it had been a way to see who amongst my peers was crossing the threshold into manhood. These days I didn't give my own armpits a second thought but I do remember a time when I'd wake up each morning to check for any sign of hair there. Because Jockey had been two years older than Brian and I, he'd been the first to sprout any hair under his arms. Then, six months later, Brian proved to be an early bloomer when he too began sporting hairy pits. My turn would not come for another eighteen months by which time both Jockey and Brian were already shaving. If puberty had been a race then it was one I had lost by a country mile.

Damian got to his feet and fossicked through the clothes on the floor, picking out a pair of baggy jeans and a grey t-shirt with a hole the size of my fist under the armpit. As he sat back down on the bed to put his shoes on, he pointed to something behind me and said, "Grab that so we can try and make some money on the way to the clinic."

I turned around and—

You've got to be fucking kidding!

He was pointing to the plastic fuel can on the floor. The one he used to dupe passersbys into giving him gas money for the fictional broke-down car he would tell them he owned.

"We should do well if you're the one asking them for the money," he said. "Pākehā boys like you have honest faces."

"The beauty of white privilege," I muttered sarcastically.

"Call it what you like, brother, but if you want me to get tested then you'll be the one asking peeps for gas money along the way."

The thought of asking total strangers for money was embarrassing, but probably no more embarrassing than what Jockey planned to talk to Damian about.

Bending over to pick up the gas can, I silently cursed my 'honest face' and the lengths I'd go to just so I could suck a dick.

Chapter 2

THE SIGHT OF JOCKEY opening the door to his sleepout in a pair of camouflage pants, tight-laced black combat boots and no shirt was all it took to know I had made the right decision bringing Damian here. That lean, summer-kissed chest of my army-obsessed master was covered in a light sheen of perspiration, dampening the fuzzy trail of hair leading below his bellybutton.

Jockey's sleepout had bottled the day's heat mercilessly. It was clogged with its usual aroma of unwashed balls and dirty socks, like the home version of a locker room. In the past the smell had made me wince and gag upon entering, now though it added to my arousal, and I wished nothing more than to sample the virile source of all these smells.

We were barely two steps inside before Damian blurted, "Mike said I can use your shower. That all good?"

"Yeah," Jockey replied. "That's all good." He pointed at the white door over near the kitchenette. "Bathroom's just through there. Help yourself to whatever towel is hanging up."

Without so much as a *thank your* or *fuck you*, Damian put down the gas cannister and swaggered his way to the bathroom, the pockets of his dirty jeans jingling with the change I'd managed to bludge from kind strangers who I'd approached with that wretched gas cannister.

Jockey fetched himself a beer from the fridge before sitting down on the couch. He then clicked his fingers, pointed to the floor in front of his feet, and said, "Sit down."

Like the obedient bitch I was becoming accustomed to being, I sat on the floor in front of his boots. Gazing up at him, I couldn't help but smile at how his small ears stuck out; a cute flaw that if he didn't shave his hair so short would be easily hidden.

"Did you boys have fun at the clinic?" he asked.

"About as much fun as can be expected from having a total stranger swab your ass and stick something in your dick hole."

He chuckled. "Did they take your blood as well?"

"Yes. I got the works. And so did Damian."

"Coolies. And did you put my number down as your contact number?"

"Yes." I very nearly hadn't, but I did as Jockey had requested.

"Let's just hope your results come back clean so we can finally make an official start to this contract."

"Yes," I agreed. "And I promise to not slip up again. The only action I'll be having until the contract starts will be with my hand."

"Don't be an idiot."

"What?"

"You don't have to go without sex, Mike. You just have to make sure its protected."

"Oh..."

"If anything I would quite like you to get fucked again before you're officially my property. Even if it's just to bring back the used rubber so I know that you're capable of using one."

"I know how to use a condom, Jockey. I'm not that special in the head."

"But have you ever used one?" Jockey smiled menacingly. "Because it seems to me that you have only ever been fucked raw."

The honest answer to that was I had used condoms plenty of times—but only ever to jerk off into. It was a phase I'd gone through when I was younger, desperate to add a bit of spice to my solo sessions. However, when it came to penetrative sex, Jockey was right—I had only ever taken it bare. The counterpoint to that was I had only ever had sex with him and Damian so it wasn't like I was a raging slut. But as he stared me down right now, judging me with those gypsy eyes of his, I must confess I did feel a tad whorish.

"How about we make that a little challenge for you over the next few days?"

"Huh?"

"I want you to have sex using a condom. Then you can bring it here and show me the proof."

"What if you fucked me with one?" I asked in my best attempt at a sexy voice. "Would that count?"

"No, bitch. I've already made it very clear my cock isn't going inside your pussy until those test results come back. You'll need to find someone else. And it can't be Damian either."

"But I don't know anyone else I could ask."

"Don't give me that excuse. You're a Hickford Homo now, Mike. Just go to the park and get your feed of dick there."

The insult only added to the fever in my balls.

"Before I forget," he said, reaching into his pocket. "I found these for you. You can start taking them from today. Had I known what a slut you'd be I would have given them to you a week ago."

"What is it?" I asked, looking at the label.

12

"It's PrEP. Pre-exposure prophylaxis. It's a drug that keeps you from getting HIV."

"Oh." I frowned.

"What's that look for?"

"I'm just wondering where you found them? And are they safe?"

"Of course they're bloody safe. I'm hardly going to poison you, dude. And I *found* them in my wardrobe. I got them a few months back for another guy who was considering becoming my faggot."

"But I though I was your first," I cringed as I quietly added, "*faggot*."

"You are. The last guy bailed before signing on the dotted line."

This was news to me, and I gotta say it sort of pissed me off. I don't suppose Jockey had lied to me but he'd certainly kept this titbit of information from me.

"Who was he?" I asked.

"Just some timewasting bitch I used to chat with online. He talked a good game but when push came to shove he couldn't walk the walk. Not like you."

I wasn't sure if he meant it as a compliment or not but I took it as one. "Thanks."

"Anyway, just make sure you start taking those pills as of today. You should reach maximum protection after seven days. Then you can get bred like a bitch all the time."

"But you just told me I have to use protection."

"You do...until the pills kick in. Making you take those is for my benefit as much as it is yours. Once the contract starts then I plan on lending your ass out on occasion to some rather sketchy dudes so it pays to play it safe."

I smoothed my long hair back, unsure of what to say to that.

The room fell silent as we looked into one another's eyes. Each second grew heavier than the last. Jockey rubbed his hand over his chest, which seemed to make the sprinkling of hair on his pecs look even darker with sweat. His smile grew before he took another sip of his beer.

Jockey ended the quiet with an order: "Take off my boots."

The weight of his words hit me in the chest. I opened my mouth, but only a few stammering sounds came out into the silence.

"Take off my boots," he repeated calmly.

After only the briefest hesitation, I untied the laces then attempted to slide the chunky footwear from his feet. After a lot of pulling, twisting and wriggling—and a little help from Jockey—the combat boots eventually slid free and the smell of his feet wafted up.

Without being told to, I took his damp socked feet into my lap, and massaged them. The spontaneous foot rub surprised us both. This wasn't something he had requested yet I felt an overwhelming need to show him my submission, and that I knew my place.

"You're going to be a very good faggot," he said, then took a quick scull on his beer.

"I hope so," I said, feeling my heart in my throat and a very distinct presence of hardness pushing at my zipper. "I want to make sure I please you."

"If you continue to do what you're told then you will make me very happy indeed."

A mindless "Yeah" was all I could summon in return. I dug my knuckle in the soft arch of his foot, earning a satisfied groan from his beer-quenched lips.

"You know that technically you don't have to follow my orders just yet, right? And you certainly don't have to rub my stinky feet." He pressed a heel into the hard mound of my crotch. "Your slutty performance with the whore last night has gifted you a few more days of freedom, remember?"

"I know."

To be honest, I hadn't intended to act so slavish so willingly, but the guilt I felt over letting Damian fuck me raw had me feeling like I owed Jockey early access to seeing me submit like this. The only thing that had me nervous was knowing Damian was just in the next room, but I figured I'd get plenty of warning from the sound of shower turning off to let go of Jockey's feet.

I continued to rub his feet, my hands absorbing the moisture of his sweaty socks. I soldiered on until eventually I heard the shower turn off. That's when my dick-fuelled bravery ended, and I promptly let go of Jockey's feet, scooting back a bit.

Jockey sniggered. "I take it someone doesn't want his whore to see him worshipping my feet?"

"Something like that," I mumbled.

Jockey finished off his beer and got up to grab himself another one when Damian finally emerged from the bathroom, a trail of mist chasing after him. He hadn't brought a change of clothes with him so was back in his grubby jeans, ripped t-shirt and that leather jacket that almost doubled as his second skin.

"Thanks for the shower, bro," Damian said. "I needed that."

"No worries," Jockey said as he peered into the fridge. "Did you fancy having a beer with me before you head off?"

"I should probably get going," Damian said.

Wonders never cease, I thought at hearing him turn down a free drink.

"Go on," Jockey said. "I've got a joint we can share to go with it."

That made Damian's brown eyes twinkle. "Sounds good to me," he said, and made his way over to the couch. Thankfully he didn't seem to find my choice of sitting on the floor odd—and if he did, he didn't question it. The other thing my former babysitter didn't question was when Jockey returned from the fridge with only two beers—one for himself and one for Damian.

Apparently my lowly status meant I was not worthy of a cold brew. And when Jockey sparked up the joint he dug of his pocket it turned out my lowly status wasn't worthy of sharing that either.

Damian wasted no time in wetting his lips. Jockey, though, made the act of drinking look pornographic. He lowered his beer bottle and pressed its cold, dew-beaded surface to his chest, between those lightly hair-dusted pectoral muscles, and slowly let the bottle slide down over his midsection, leaving a shimmery trail of wiped-off moisture, until he held it at his crotch, subtly hunching his hips back and forth, as though the beer bottle were his big prick and he was jacking it for my pleasure.

After a while, a thin layer of smoke hovered as Jockey and Damian got stoned on the couch, talking like old friends catching up. As they gasbagged with each other, ignoring my existence, I let my gaze hover over Jockey's camo-patterned bulge. I imagined the rasp of his zipper the next time he pulled it down to unleash his cock—secretly hoping it would be to fuck me again.

My inner battle with submission continued to confuse me. A part of me still resented being cast in the role of Jockey's faggot, another part of me craved that thick cock of his with every fibre of my being.

Accompanying my tug-of-war with submission was the uneasy knowledge of knowing I was in a room with two men who had both fucked me. While it made me feel like a slut, especially since they'd both bred me like a bitch, there was a thrill in knowing I knew what lay beneath the crotch of each man's pants. Damian Takarangi and Jockey Savage had similarities—a love of pot, booze, and cocky personalities—but the size of their cocks and smell of their balls were not similar. Nor were their techniques. Despite Damian being almost ten years older than the scruffy stoner, Jockey was hands down the better fuck.

I kept glancing at Jockey's crotch, especially each time he reached down to give his balls a scratch. A familiar darkness started to thicken in my chest, its tendrils spilling into my every vein. Rational thought began to leave my body through every clammy pore. *If Damian wasn't here right now I'd totally beg you to let me suck your cock.* And that thought confirmed what I had suspected—my battle with submission was going to be a losing one.

"What's that?" Damian asked, in the choke-voiced croak of a person holding in pot smoke. He let the smoke out slowly, pointing at something behind me. "That thing over there."

I turned to look in the direction of Damian's outstretched finger. My stomach dropped when I saw what he was pointing to. It was the pair of Calvin Kleins I had worn the night Jockey had fucked me for the first time. Maybe it was because I was used to them being there that I hadn't noticed just how damn eye-catching they were, especially with the way Jockey had positioned them so that they were inside-out with the ass-end on display with its stains of dry cum.

"Those are Mike's cummy knickers," Jockey answered.

The room fell silent.

And it lingered, cold and icy, like a frozen blade.

Finally, in a very slow, low voice, Damian said, "Why are they hanging above *your* bed?" When he didn't get a response, Damian turned to me and asked the same question. "Why are your undies hanging above *his* bed?"

I shrugged and tried a tiny laugh.

Jockey looked at me, as if seeking permission for a confession. I shook my head. But he ignored it by responding, "Because Mike is my faggot."

"Ya fucking what?" Damian's shocked voice rang around the sleepout.

"Mike is my faggot," Jockey said again. "I own him. Or at least I will do soon. He signed a contract."

Chapter 3

FOR THE NEXT FIVE MINUTES words like *bitch, faggot, slave* and *sub* were thrown around generously, their meaning all the same, as Jockey attempted to explain to Damain about the contract I had signed. Damian's brown face was wrinkled with confusion, the bushy brows crinkling, as he listened to Jockey but stared at me. And slowly he began to understand, although I could tell that it was the last thing in the world he had ever expected. His thickly lashed eyes became lucid and penetrating, and then he bent his head in order not to look at me at all.

"So that's it," Damian said finally, deliberately, when Jockey had finished talking. "You signed a contract that gives another man ownership of you? And you signed it willingly?"

Everything within me wanted to scream out with fury and pain and denial, yet, at the same time, I felt a tingling excitement stirring down in my groin—an excitement which made me despise myself.

"Yes, sir," I said, the word slipping out.

Damian laughed, mocking me with his eyes. "What the fuck, Mike? I've known you since you were how old? You were raised to have more brains than this. Where's your mana?"

I wanted to call him out for his hypocrisy and own lack of self-respect, but I knew there was a difference between us. Damian cheapened himself to get by, did what he thought he had to do, but at no point did a man own him after the fun had ended. My former babysitter could leave each of those situations knowing he was his own person and do what he wanted to do. That wasn't an option for me.

Damian laughed some more then turned his attention back to Jockey. "I don't know whether to congratulate you or punch you."

"I think I'd prefer your congratulations," Jockey said with a smile.

"Well, congratulations. I've heard of kinky shit like this before, stuff I've seen on the internet, but I've never come across it in real life. And to think of all people its little Michael Freeman who gave his ass up to be owned."

"To be fair, Mike isn't officially my property for another week. But then he will be." Jockey flashed me a grin, the effect marred by the fact he was taking a drag on the joint. "Go grab me and Damian another beer each. That's a good bitch."

Calling me a *good bitch* was just Jockey showing off but he got the desired effect when Damian cracked up in a fit of giggles.

I fetched them their drinks and took my seat on the floor again.

"Are you gay?" Damian asked our stoner host. He asked it as one might ask about the weather.

"Nar, not really. I just live by the philosophy any hole's a goal."

"We probably have that in common."

"I think there's something else we have in common" Jockey said.

"What's that?" Damian leaned back and belched.

"Mike." Jockey gestured with his bottle, pointing the bottom of it at me. "We've both fucked him."

"He told you about that, did he?" The sneer my former babysitter gave me made my balls shrink. "I thought we had agreed that stays between us?"

"I, uh..."

"It's not Mike's fault," Jockey said, cutting me off. "He came here last night to have his pussy inspected and I saw it was full of cum so I made him tell me who had fucked him."

"What else has he told you?"

"He said that you're the best fuck he's ever had. Said he can't stop thinking about how good your dick felt in his pussy."

"I only fucked him just last night."

"Yeah, but I think it's safe to say you've left quite the lasting impression. He thinks your dick is amazing."

Rather than question the bullshit story, Damian sat back with a smug grin on his face. He widened his legs, like he wanted to drag attention to his supposedly *amazing* dick. "I guess I've had lotsa practise. Know how to give it to them how they want it."

"That's pretty much what Mike told me last night." Jockey shot me a wink. "That's what you said, wasn't it? That Damian is a man who knows how to fuck an ass just right?"

Hesitantly, I responded, "Yeah... that's what I said."

Damian nodded, still looking smug. "Yep. I may not be the smartest Māori on the marae, but I sure have learned how to fuck."

"Which is why I have a favour to ask you," Jockey said.

Damian's eyes narrowed, stoned and thoughtful. "What sort of favour?"

"I understand that for the right price you offer certain services."

Damian cast me a side-eye full of animosity. "You really did run your mouth didn't you, bitch? If I'da known you couldn't keep your trap shut, I wouldn't have agreed to do it."

My former babysitter had every right to be pissed at me. We had agreed to not tell anyone about the night I paid him for sex, and even though he'd gone on to assault me and mug me, I couldn't help but feel I was the traitor in this scenario.

"Don't be too hard on him," Jockey said. "You know what faggots are like. They've got big mouths and tiny cocks."

Damian snorted. "Sounds about right."

Jockey nudged me with his foot. "Go sit outside for a while. The men need to talk business."

How fucking rude, I thought, but I got to my feet as if my muscles were making decisions independently of my brain. Just as I was about to close the door behind me, I heard Jockey say, "Good boy."

Being complimented like a dog who'd fetched a stick should have bothered me. But somehow, getting any sort of praise from Jockey meant something. It meant enough to me that I sat outside quite happily, eavesdropping to the conversation going on inside.

It was hard to hear what was being said but I picked up enough to make out that Jockey was showing Damian the contract I had signed and explaining to Damian my role as an owned faggot. Naturally, this made Damian laugh—quickly followed by him worriedly asking Jockey, "You don't want me to sign something like this, do you? Cause I won't. I don't mind doing jobs like this on the downlow but no man owns Damian Takarangi. I got way too much pride for that."

"Nah, man," Jockey replied. "I just wanted you to be aware of the situation with Mike."

"Okay," Damian said.

"The thing with faggots, especially new ones like Mike, is that their pussies are insatiable to begin with. Once they get a taste for dick they can't get enough of it. Which is why I was hoping you and I could have an arrangement where you fuck him for me a couple times a week. Help keep his pussy happy and well-fed."

If I were Damian I would have laughed again but he simply replied with, "I see. And you'd pay me for each time I fuck him?"

"I would."

"How much?"

"There are a couple ways we could—"

Suddenly, a car with a fucked exhaust pipe sped past, killing my ability to listen to what was being said inside the sleepout. By the time the noisy vehicle was gone, Jockey and Damian had lowered their voices and I couldn't make out what was being said.

As I waited to be let back inside, I wondered how Gavin's night with Fiona and Stryder had gone. I hadn't seen him since yesterday but Jockey had let enough slip to me last night that suggested Stryder had not cancelled on the threeway like he'd promised me he would after I'd paid the wayward teen fifty bucks.

It probably served me right. I should have known better than to try and cut deals with boys who sell their asses in public toilets. Mind you, that was exactly what Jockey was trying to do right now with Damian—cut a deal. I just hoped the redneck stoner had better luck than I'd had so far.

I could only assume that whatever Jockey was trying to do was part of his plan to get vengeance against Damian for ripping me off and beating my face with that overpriced dildo I had bought. A part of me felt bad for luring Damian here, but a bigger part of me was flattered to think Jockey would try and avenge my honour...which was funny when you considered Jockey liked to remind me I had no honour. But still...it was sort of sweet to think I had someone keen to protect me, even if it was being done in what so far seemed a sordid manner.

"You can come back in now, bitch," Jockey hollered from inside.

Stepping back inside the sleepout, I found Jockey rummaging through a bedside drawer while Damian sat on Jockey's couch with his legs in full man-spread mode. The discussion in my absence had left them both with very different looks on their faces: Jockey was all smiles whereas Damian's lips appeared to ripple with something like disgust.

Returning to my spot on the floor, I watched as Jockey pulled a wad of cash out of the drawer—way more cash than I would have expected my stoner pal to have in his possession—and flashed it about like a cheerleader holding up a pompom.

I was tempted to call him an idiot for making such a show of it, especially for doing so in front of a known thief like Damian. Just when I thought Jockey's stupidity couldn't be get any worse, he opened the next drawer down and pulled out a plastic bag containing—

Oh my fuck! That better not be what I think it is.

Dangling the bag like he was holding the tail of a dead mouse, Jockey said, "And if you'd rather be paid in crack then that can be arranged."

Granted, I wasn't the most knowledgeable when it came to illegal substances but I was pretty fucking sure there was enough crack in that bag for Jockey to find himself in some very deep shit if he was busted.

"How have you got so much of that?" Damian's druggy eyes lit up. "Are you dealing?"

"That's a very good question," I said, sounding like a school principal. "Are you dealing, Jockey?"

"Tell me something, Michael." Jockey said my name with all the contempt of a slur. "Weren't you told to keep your dicksucker shut unless spoken to?"

"Yes but—"

"No buts, bitch. This is not a conversation for faggots." He then turned his attention to Damian. "So what's your preferred poison, bro? Cash or crack? As you can see I've got plenty of both."

Damian looked like all his Christmases had come at once. "Can I try some of it first? Gotta make sure it's good stuff if I'm gonna opt for that as payment."

"No," Jockey said firmly, putting the bag of drugs back into the drawer. "You can have some on Friday before the job if you like. If you decide it ain't up to scratch after we're done then I'll just pay you with the cash instead."

Damian nodded, rubbing sweaty palms down the legs of his pants. "Sounds good."

How the fuck had I not known my stoner pal was dealing drugs? It left me with an awful feeling in my stomach, one that made me seriously consider running out the door and telling Jockey our contract was over before it had a chance to start.

Jockey went and sat back down beside Damian. "So we will see you there midnight Friday?"

Damian nodded. He picked at his nose with a dirty fingernail. "Midnight Friday."

"What's happening midnight on Friday?" I asked.

"Your master wants to watch us fuck. At the pig pen."

Hearing someone else refer to Jockey as my master was strange. But I suppose that's what he was, or that's what he would be once the contract started.

I turned to Jockey. "You want to watch us have sex at Hickford Park?"

There was a hint of a menacing smile on his lips. "You told me so much about how great last night was that I'm keen to see the scene reenacted."

The shifty fucker didn't need us to reenact the scene for him because he'd been there. Not that Damian knew that, of course.

"You don't have to do it if you don't want to," Jockey said to me; voice sweet, eyes anything but. "Neither of you do. I'm all about consent and freewill."

Bullshit!

"We'll do it," Damian said gruffly. "I need the cash and by the sounds of it your faggot needs my cock again."

I didn't appreciate Damian's tone, or choice of words.

"Is it safe for us to do that though?" I asked. "Won't there be people there?"

"The pigpen is dead by midnight," Damian said. "The only people in the park will be desperados loitering by the loos. No one will bother us."

"Are you sure?"

"Of course I'm fucking sure," Damian snapped. "I wouldn't agree to do it otherwise."

"I hope it's a good, long fuck," Jockey said. "Want to make sure I am getting my money's worth."

"Don't you worry, you'll get your money's worth," Damian said. "Mike might have told you this already, but I pride myself on my customer service."

I was tempted to ask since when did physical assault and theft constitute customer service, but I remained quiet.

"I'm looking forward to it," Jockey said to Damian before turning his attention to me. "Damian has also very kindly agreed to fuck you at least twice a week once your contract starts. Isn't that nice of him?"

When I saw Jockey wink discreetly, I faked a smile and nodded. "It is. Very nice of him."

Had Damian not been so busy staring at the drawers containing the drugs and cash then he would have seen how forced my excitement was. His attention was swiftly brought back to the moment at hand when Jockey said, "Do you mind if I check out the merch?"

"What?" Damian looked confused.

"Do you mind if I check out the merch?" Jockey asked again, his hand hovering over Damian's crotch.

A flitter of annoyance passed before Damian's eyes. "Knock yourself out," he eventually said, albeit reluctantly. He placed his hands behind his head, slid down a little, and spread his legs.

I watched in horny horror as Jockey lowered his hand and started groping Damian's denim-clad crotch. Jockey let out a satisfied *mmm* and groped a little harder.

The scene was reminiscent of the night I had hired Damian for sex, but unlike the nervous wreck I had been Jockey was cool, calm and collected. He didn't appear to be in any rush either, happily groping Damian through the denim material.

As for Damian, he too seemed more relaxed than he had been when I had molested his junk. Was Jockey a more calming influence, or was it the pot?

"Stand up and unzip your pants," Jockey ordered in a voice which sounded strangely husky, not bothering to make it a request this time. "I wanna see the cock that drives my faggot so wild."

Damian stood, and he didn't look terribly happy, but he unbuttoned the fly of his jeans. He hesitated, reaching into the darkness behind them before pulling out his dick with a quick flick of his fingers. Despite the fondle he'd just received Damian's dick was still soft, drooping downward, dark foreskin peeled back from the head.

Jockey knelt on the floor, his face becoming level with Damian's crotch. Smiling at the flaccid member, he undid the button holding up Damian's jeans and tugged them down so that they rested just above the Māori man' knees. He then did the same to the boxer shorts, leaving Damian's junk and bare ass exposed.

"You can suck it if you want," Damian said, sounding more confident than he looked.

Jockey appeared to give the offer serious consideration but instead he just kept staring at the pale brown dick inches in front of his face. This silent observation went on for quite some time until finally Jockey rose to his full height and stirred the air with his index finger—a *turn around* gesture.

Damian turned around slowly, showing Jockey his ass.

Jockey grabbed hold of one fuzzy butt cheek, gripping Damian's ass meat tightly. I recognised the look on my master's face. It was the same look he'd had both times he had fucked me. It was animal instinct mingled with raw lust; the visible sign of dominant urges and dark needs living somewhere between his brain and his balls.

Watching Damian's ass jiggle in Jockey's hand, I was reminded how my former babysitter had let himself go. Once upon a time that ass would have been rock-hard but now it was every bit as average as the rest of his drug-fucked body. Average or not, I still wanted to fuck Damian, just so I could say I had.

When he'd had enough of checking out Damian's ass, Jockey sat back down on the couch and said, "Have a seat, Damian, and let the faggot suck you off."

"What?" I hadn't expected that.

"Am I speaking Swahili or something?" Jockey turned the full glare of his predator grin on me. "I just told you to suck this man's dick. Now get to it."

Damian sat down and we exchanged glances. He looked less than enthused at the offer of a free blowie, but he didn't stop me when I crawled towards him and dragged his jeans and boxers from his knees down to his ankles.

What am I doing? Why am I doing this? Even as I asked those questions, I closed my lips around his limp meat and started sucking. His skin tasted clean and fruity from whatever bodywash he'd used in Jockey's shower, and his pubes were still damp. I tangled my fingers in the curls, then grabbed hold of his balls, squeezing gently while I sucked his cock.

Jockey may have been sitting just a couple feet away, completely uninvolved, but he was the one with the power. The one who was breaking me down, stealing my dignity, reminding me I was his possession.

I'm a faggot, I told myself. *Jockey's faggot.*

As I sucked Damian's cock, I delicately stroked his balls with my fingertips. His shaft was completely rigid now, and his hands were gripping the seat of the couch. I glanced up at him; his eyes were closed tight in concentration. I rubbed his thigh with my other hand and continued to work on him with my mouth, up and down, up and down.

"Yeah, that's it, bitch," Jockey growled. "Show Damian what a good little cocksucker you are."

Something in my chest ached like a hunger that was being fed. It felt good to give in. To accept my place beneath that of men more worthy than myself. I was behaving like some cock-hungry skank, taking my former babysitter's dick in my throat, giving him pleasure. Tasting him. All the way down, all the way up. Slow and steady. Wet sucking sounds announcing what a slut I was.

Damian's moans were little more than gasping grunts. I stared up at him through blurry eyes. I must have looked pathetic or whorish. Probably both. The look he gave back was one I had grown familiar with these past few weeks—contempt. My mouth was little more than a cunt of convenience as far as he was concerned.

I slurped my mouth off his cock and lowered my head to lick his testicles, pulled them gently into my mouth, circled them with my tongue. I worked my way back up to his brown shaft and licked its length, then took him back into my mouth and all the way down, back into my hot throat. And all the way up. And again. And again.

"He is actually pretty good at this," Damian said with a shudder.

"Are you gonna come soon?" Jockey asked him.

"I can do if you want."

"Do it, man. I want you to feed my bitch a load. Send him home with sperm breath."

Damian grabbed my head, fingers twining in my blond locks, and started thrusting his hips, fucking my face like it was a pussy. The couch squeaked at his bucking and squirming.

It was hard to catch my breath between thrusts as Damian smashed his pelvis with increasing force into my face. The wiry hairs above his cock were each a weapon at these speeds, scratching my lips and nose, battering my cheeks.

Damian gave no warning. Didn't need to. We all knew I was the bitch in this scenario. He just thrust upward to drive his spasming cock deep into me as the first burst of cum came out, then again with the second.

It was a humbling experience, being fed the contents of his balls. After last night's brutal buggering, and now this, I would never be able to hold my head high in Damian's presence ever again. He may have only been a beta male according to Jockey but this drug-fucked beneficiary was now miles above me when it came to the hierarchy of men.

More cum poured out, filling my mouth, feeding my stomach. I swallowed every hot drop of seed he gave me, letting his orgasm run its course. Finally, I heard him take a deep breath and exhale.

Damian's body relaxed. My hair was no longer pulled. The guy's entire stance seemed to weaken. Slowly, my head slid away. The velvety tip pulled free of my lips and Damian's slimy cock fell back between his thighs.

I licked my excess saliva from his shaft and glanced up at him. He was looking back down at me now, his eyes half-lidded.

"Thanks," he said between breaths.

Even if I wanted to respond, I had no words to offer. My eyes darted from Jockey's smirking face to the lump of limp dick between Damian's thighs. I could still see how wet it was from my spit.

Damian reached beside the couch to the floor and fetched something. His beer. I watched him put the bottle to his lips and begin to chug the remnants. When he'd finished he leaned forward to pull his pants back up but Jockey's authoritative voice put a stop to that.

"Keep them down," said my master. "I like looking at your cock."

Damian's confidence faltered for a fraction of a second and he saw me seeing. He leaned back and sat there fully exposed, soft brown prick dribbling jizz remnants onto his inner thigh.

Jockey got up, fetched his cigarettes and an ash tray, lit one for him and one for Damian, and sat back beside him with the ash tray on Damian's shirt-covered belly. If my former babysitter had an issue with being used like a table then he kept it to himself.

They smoked in silence for a few minutes, Jockey playing idly with Damian's spent cock, saying nothing. It was as if I wasn't even there. Just a mute witness to this bizarre affection.

"I like you," Jockey said finally, rubbing one socked-foot up and down Damian's shin. "You're a cool cunt."

"So are you, bro," Damian returned with a smile.

"I'm gonna jack off the moment you leave, just thinking about Mike sucking your dick."

"You like jerking off?"

"Hell, yes. Don't you?"

Damian laughed. "Yeah, bro. I like to jerk off."

"Perhaps I can watch you masturbate sometime. I'd like that."

With the edge of the ash tray, Damian made the tip of his cigarette into a neat, orange cone. "That can be arranged. For the right price."

"An affordable one I hope."

Damian took a deep drag and blew smoke out slowly. Then he laughed. "Yeah, bro. I'll make sure it's affordable."

"Random question," Jockey said, "but could you ever see yourself dating another man?"

Damian's response was short and sharp. "Nope."

"What if the dude was rich? Like a sugar daddy type."

Damian shook his head, with a faint, curious light in his eyes. Then he dismissed the idea. "Nar, that's still too queer for me," he said, and stubbed out his cigarette. "I'm like ninety percent into bitches. The other ten per cent I just use to make me some cash."

To Damian's credit, that sounded a pretty honest response.

"So you wouldn't be interested in becoming an owned faggot like Mike?" Jockey asked, like he was fishing for secrets.

"No way. I've got way too much mana for that. Plus I ain't fucked in the head."

"That's a shame."

Damian smiled. "You like me that much, huh?"

"It's not that. It's your dick." Jockey squeezed the flaccid brown member. "It's small like Mike's."

"It's small cos it's soft, bro."

"I know, but even when you were hard it wasn't *that* big."

"Say what?"

"I'm not saying it's a micro penis or nuffin, but it ain't the biggest tool in the shed. Even you gotta admit that?"

Things were suddenly feeling tense again; in my awkwardness, I glanced around the room, trying to look natural. How the fuck did

Jockey possibly think that telling a guy like Damian he had a small dick was a good idea. It was asking for trouble.

Damian ran a thumb under his nose. "You know, bro, if we weren't about to go into business then saying shit like that would get you a punch."

"Would it?" Jockey poked the bear by tugging on Damian's limp penis. "But it turns me on telling men with small cocks how small they are."

"I s'pose we all got our kinks," Damian grumbled.

"I reckon if a guy is on the small side, like you both are, he should just accept it and let his asshole become a pussy."

"What the fuck?" Damian snorted. "I ain't got a pussy."

"You know what I mean though. Ass, mouth, pussy, cunt. Anything that takes a dick is the same thing."

"I s'pose so."

"I heard that if a guy gets fucked hard and deep enough, and on the right angle, he can train his ass to orgasm like a pussy."

I expected Damian to laugh again. I know that's what I wanted to do. But my former babysitter surprised me by very calmly responding, "You're taking about cunting."

Jockey's eyes lit up. "So you've heard of it?"

Damian nodded. "Yeah. I've seen it happen a few times at Hickford Park. The fag gets bummed so hard and deep he goes all funny. It looks freaky, and they act weird afterwards. Really fucking weird."

"Weird how?" I asked, forgetting my oath of silence.

"It's hard to say," Damian replied. "But it changes them. Makes them even hungrier for cock."

"That tells you how good it must feel," Jockey said, pointing his comment at Damian. "Wouldn't you want to experience that?"

Damian stared at him as if Jockey were from outer space, and didn't dignify the question with an answer.

"I've always wanted to cunt a faggot," Jockey said. "But I've never really had the opportunity."

"How come?" Damian asked.

"Until Mike I've never had a guy I can fuck as much as I like. And I know it takes some effort to get a faggot cunted. Maybe even more inches than I have to offer."

"Is this your way of admitting you're actually the one with a little dick?" Damian sniggered, sounding very much like he enjoyed saying that.

"No," Jockey said flatly.

"So do you think you'll try and cunt Mike?" Damian asked. His smirk made my balls shrink.

They both stared at me like I was an insect under a microscope. It was an unnerving, mostly because I had no idea what cunting actually was.

"Maybe," Jockey said, sounding less keen on the idea than I had assumed he would be. "But I'd feel bad because Mike was my mate before becoming my faggot. And I don't suppose that's the sort of thing a guy should do to his mates."

"Agreed," Damian said.

Just as quickly as the topic of cunting had arisen it was forgotten about, and Jockey started telling us about how he was going away overnight with his aunt and uncle to visit his aunt's brother Ralph who was dying of cancer. I had never heard of this Ralph relative before but then that may have been because I'd never taken much interest in Jockey before he had fucked me. Now I made a mental note to ask him later about his sick relative.

"It's a total pain in the ass," Jockey said, lighting up a cigarette. "but my aunt reckons Ralph ain't got long left, said it might be the last chance I get to see him alive, so I guess I better go say goodbye to the old codger."

"Whanau's important, bro," Damian said. "So it's probably best you go see him while you can."

"Yeah, you're right."

"When will youse get back?" Damian asked.

"Ralph lives all the way up in Kaitaia so we won't get back until sometime tomorrow night." Jockey took a deep drag on the cigarette then passed it to Damian. "So it's pretty safe to say I'll be knackered for work on Monday." Jockey finally let go of Damian's dick then kneaded about his own groin. "I'm busting for a piss."

"Thanks for sharing," Damian sniggered.

Sighing like a man already stood on a urinal, Jockey said, "I was wondering if you'd mind helping me go."

"Helping you what?" Damian frowned. "Help you take a piss?"

"Yeah. I thought you cold drink it. Mike said you do that sort of thing."

An imaginary alarm went off in my brain. *DANGER! DANGER! DANGER!* What exactly did Jockey think he was up to? This was insane, and another instance of Jockey putting me in the shit with my former babysitter and onetime whore.

Damian flashed me the evils. "Mike needs to learn to keep his waha shut."

"Come on, man." Jockey palmed his crotch. "I want Mike to watch a professional do it. That way he can learn how to do it himself."

"It ain't fucking rocket science. You just swallow."

"I know but I'd still like him to watch and learn. Maybe you could give him some pointers so he doesn't spit any on me when he tries it."

"That shit costs."

"Come on...surely you can let your new business partner have one on the house?"

Surely this would be the moment that Damian would just tell Jockey to go fuck himself. But that's not what happened. With his jeans still snagged at his ankles, Damian dropped to the floor beside me and turned to face Jockey. "Okay," he said, "but next time I expect some cash. Got it?"

"Got it." Jockey pinched the tag of his zipper, drew it down with a rasp that seemed deafening then fished out his flaccid cock.

Was I missing something? Had my master been using hypnosis without me realising? Or was he a master salesman, capable of selling ice to polar bears. It was as puzzling as it was enlightening.

I was a little jealous that Damian was getting the chance to wrap his lips around Jockey's cock. Mind you, the fact piss was about to come out of it was a major mood killer. But I knew it was only a matter of time before I'd be forced to do the same. But Damian wasn't being forced. The idiot was choosing to do it.

Damian turned to me like a teacher. "So first you gotta put in your mouth. Not too far back. Start with the tip at the entrance. You don't want it in too deep in case he spurts hard and hits the back of your throat and makes you cough. The last thing you want is the piss to dribble out."

"Are you listening, Mike?" Jockey snapped when he caught me staring at his dick.

"Yes, sir."

Damian waited for Jockey to nod before continuing with the lesson. "Most guys going for a piss start small and build up. So that helps. The trick is trying to gauge the rhythm of the spurts. You wanna be in sync with the flow. A bit like dancing to a beat."

I nodded.

"It's often easier when the dude is erect because he is less likely to let rip like a firehose. When a man's flaccid, and you will know this yourself, it can be hard to switch off the flow when it starts. That's where you need to tap him on the thigh or something. Or hum over his cock. If you remember that's what I did when I drank yours."

I nodded again.

Jockey suddenly rose to his full height, aimed his dick at Damian's face, and said, "Shall we get this show on the road? I'm fucking busting."

Damian nodded and assumed the urinal position; on his knees, mouth agape.

Jockey placed the soft tip of his dick over Damian's tongue. They made eye contact and Damian shifted forward slightly, clutching Jockey's hips for balance. Nearly ten seconds passed before Jockey let out a gentle sigh and I saw Damian's jaw tic.

The flow had begun.

Jockey's piss gurgled hollowly in Damian's gaping mouth, and I watched the Māori man swallow Jockey's liquid offering, his Adam's apple bobbing as he gulped. He struggled occasionally as the flood of piss from Jockey's cock continued to fill his mouth faster than he could swallow. Each time that happened his long fingers tapped Jockey's hip and he made a soft humming sound. Jockey would stop pissing, give his human urinal time to catch up, then start the flow back up.

It went on for quite a while, this start-stop leak, and I'm sure it left Damain with an awfully full belly of warm beer piss. When Jockey's flow finally came to an end, Damian suckled the tip of his cock clean, and then Jockey pushed him away.

"Cheers for that, Damian," Jockey said, then casually put his cock away. "I can't wait until Mike is all trained up to be my personal piss pig. The nights he stays over I won't even have to get out of bed to use the toilet. I can just piss in his mouth and go back to sleep. How awesome will that be?"

"Pretty awesome," Damian mumbled, wiping dry his piss-stained lips.

"I'm gonna need you fellas to bugger off now," Jockey said abruptly. "I've got to start packing for my trip. I'll text you both when I get back from visiting Ralph and we can go over our plans for next Friday."

Damian replied with that most Kiwi of sayings, "Sweet as, bro." He wasted no time pulling up his jeans, buttoning them up, and rushing out the door.

I held back, lingering, wanting to speak with Jockey in private.

"What are you still doing here?" said Jockey when Damian had left and I hadn't. "I told you to go home."

"I wanted to talk with you about—" *why you have drugs in our bedside drawer.*

"I'm busy, Mike," Jockey snapped, cutting me off midsentence. "I'll see you when I get back. Okay?"

"But you promised me a load of cum if I brought Damian over." I sounded like a sulky child who had missed out on a lollipop.

"Yes, and Damian gave you a huge mouthful. Which means I kept my promise."

Technically he wasn't wrong, I guess.

He patted my cheek. "Now go on home," he urged. "I have a lot to organise before my trip."

With my tongue burning from unasked questions, I turned and left, leaving Jockey in peace.

Chapter 4

WHILE GAVIN BUZZED around the house like a blue-assed fly, I commandeered the couch by sprawling out on it and watching reruns of Kath & Kim on the television. I'd been home for over an hour and so far my stepfather had made no mention about what had happened the night before, nothing about Fiona or Stryder. It was almost like his threeway hadn't happened, but of course it had, and I kept catching myself looking at his ass and imagining Stryder's young cock breaking the seal.

The nosy bitch lurking in my conscience wanted to ask Gavin what it had been like, to hear how he felt about taking a cock inside him for the first time, but I knew better than to pry.

Not only had Gavin not brought it up, he just wasn't saying much in general. Normally he would chew my ear off the moment I walked in the door but today he was communicating in grunts and nods, coming in and out of the lounge as if he couldn't be in one place for longer than a minute. In the words of the foxy ladies from Fountain Lake whom I was watching, he was acting *different and ewesual*. Clearly Gavin was in a bad mood, like he was regretting going through with it. I felt bad for him, but I had warned him not to do it.

About an hour later, Gavin reappeared in the lounge. The red shorts he had on looked new, so did the blue Adidas top he wore. *Gifts from Fiona perhaps?* What didn't look quite so new were the scuffed black trainers on his feet.

"I'm heading out for a while," he said, avoiding my gaze. "I'll grab us something for dinner on the way home."

"Sounds good. Where are you going?"

"Just out," he replied cryptically. The muscles rippled on his hairy calf as he turned to leave, tendons tensing all the way down to his sock-less trainers.

I didn't see Gavin again until dinner time when he returned home with a bag full of groceries and two chicken salads he'd picked up from Subway. It seemed an odd choice for dinner, I thought. Our usual fast-food fix was Maccas or a bucket of greasy chicken pieces from KFC. But I wasn't about to complain about the free meal—even if it did little to ignite my taste buds.

Sat at the dinner table, we didn't talk and he avoided meeting my gaze. Whatever bee was in his bonnet was still there and I didn't fancy getting stung by it. But there was only so long I could sit in silence and pretend everything was normal, so after a few more minutes I thought *fuck it*, I was going to ask him what had happened.

"How was last night," I asked quietly. But my words felt loud between us.

He looked at me, finally, his eyes crashing into mine.

"I guess last night must have been pretty intense," I added.

Gavin said nothing, but he shook his head a little. I couldn't tell if he was agreeing or disagreeing.

"At least, you don't have to keep wearing the chastity cage," I ventured.

Gavin still said nothing.

"You're not still wearing it...are you?"

He laughed a little, but didn't look like he found the question funny. "I think we can find better things to talk about than my penis."

"Sorry." I stabbed my fork at the plate, shovelling a bland mouthful of lettuce into my mouth. "So where did you go to earlier?"

"Hmm?" He looked at me, one eyebrow quirked. "What was that?"

"Where did you go earlier? You were gone ages."

"I went and signed up at the gym."

"The gym?" It was my turn to raise an eyebrow. "For real?"

"Yes for real." He peeled off the blue Adidas jumper he'd still been wearing, revealing a baggy white t-shirt marked with dark pit stains. "I had a real good work out too."

"Why the hell would you bother joining a gym?"

"Why do you think? So I can get in shape. It's time I start taking better care of myself and tone up a bit."

Suddenly the salad for dinner made sense.

"You don't need the gym," I said. "You're in perfect shape."

"I'm really not. I've got no abs."

"You haven't had abs for years so what's that matter?"

"It just does," he said icily.

Knowing better than to poke the bear, I went and put my half-finished salad in the fridge. Turning around, after shutting the fridge door, I saw how the bag of groceries Gavin had bought were dangerously close to falling from the kitchen bench onto the floor. My stepfather's constant putting off of doing his turn at the dishes meant bench space was minimal. I went to push the bag back so it was at less risk of falling victim to gravity. While doing so, I glanced inside the bag of groceries in the hope I might find something with a few more calories and taste.

Gavin sprung up from his chair. "Don't look in the bag!"

Too-fucking-late-dot-com.

"What the hell?" I muttered as I locked eyes on the contents inside. There was no food inside the bag. Just jars of multivitamins and what appeared to be every type of moisturizer known to man. Turning back to look at Gavin, I asked, "Is there a reason you bought half the fucking beauty aisle home with you?"

He looked embarrassed. "It's a long story."

"Is it?"

"Not really actually." He sat back down. "Just a short and embarrassing one."

I was intrigued so I returned to the table and waited for him to spill.

With a sheepish look, Gavin said, "You know how I was supposed to be having that threesome last night, right?"

"Yeah?"

"Well... it didn't go ahead."

"Oh." I was confused, and strangely relieved. "So you didn't..."

"My back passage is still a virgin." He was trying to be funny but his smile was woeful.

"But what's that got to do with you suddenly having a midlife crisis?"

"I'm not having a midlife crisis. I'm just concerned about my appearance."

"Because?"

"Because..." He took a deep breath before continuing. "The reason the threeway didn't go ahead is because Stryder told Fiona he decided I was too old and ugly to hook up with."

I could see Gavin's jaw tick; the words painful for him to say. They would have been painful for anyone to say about themselves, but especially for a man who was, albeit downplayed, quite a vain fucker.

My relief over him not biting the pillow for a teenage whore was swiftly replaced with guilt. Tremendous guilt. This was my fault. *Fucking Stryder!* Yes I had wanted pouty-lipped blond to cancel the threeway, but not with an excuse that would left Gavin feeling ugly and rejected.

"I'm sure Stryder didn't mean it that way," I said.

"I think you'll find that he did. He said as much in the text message he sent to Fiona."

What Stryder had done wasn't cool, but I was a bit puzzled by Gavin letting Stryder's opinion impact him to the extent he had joined the gym.

"Let me get this straight, excuse the pun. You, a *straight* man, are upset that another male doesn't want to sleep with you?"

"His gender has nothing to do with it. It's the fact the little fucker said I'm old and hideous. But I suppose he isn't wrong. To a lad his age I'm probably like the Crypt Keeper"

"Stop being so dramatic. You look fine."

"I'm not being dramatic. It's the truth. I'm getting past it." He sighed. "The gym and moisturisers might help for a while but I suppose I am only delaying the inevitable."

"What are you on about? You were a handsome dude when I met you, you're still a handsome dude, and you're dating one

45

of the best-looking women in town, and I imagine you'll still be ridiculously handsome when you're fifty."

That made him smile. Briefly.

There was a pause, a solid five seconds of silence on his end, then, "Thanks, Mike. But it doesn't count coming from you."

"Excuse me?" I forced a casualness into my voice, belying my desire to reach across the table and slap some sense into him. "Why doesn't it count?"

"Because we're whanau. You're obliged to tell me I'm pretty."

I laughed. "I don't think I would ever use the word pretty to describe you. Those punga legs of yours would look tragic in a dress."

"Speaking of dresses, maybe I should buy one made of paper bags and put it over my face."

He followed his response up with laughter to insinuate he was joking, but I knew Gavin well enough to know he wasn't finding any of it funny. He was hurt. Hurting badly. And it was all my fault.

What do I do?

It wasn't like I could go back to Stryder and tell him to come up with a new excuse. That would make Gavin and Fiona suspicious. It would also run the risk of the threeway then going ahead. And I still did not believe it was a good idea for Gavin to let a teenage hustler fuck him.

"My opinion should count considering I used to have a crush on you." My voice came out hoarse, almost a whisper.

"What?"

"I used to have a crush on you. You know...when I was younger."

Gavin's mouth pulled to the side in a sceptical sneer. "Bullshit. Stop trying to make me feel better."

"It's true. You were the first guy I ever—" I quickly stopped myself from finishing that sentence.

"First guy you ever what?"

"It doesn't matter."

"Nar, tell me."

"You were the first guy I ever thought about while having a *wank*." I whispered the last word while making a tossing gesture with my hand.

"Really?" A broad grin rose on his stubbly face. "So your feet weren't lying when they said you have a thing for us Māori boys."

"Last time I checked I didn't have feet that could talk."

"I'm talking about those messages your sexy vampire wrote on them." He began smirking. "The ones that said you love Māori—"

I was quick to cut him off. "I know what they said."

"So I'm the one that started that trend, aye?"

I laughed, wanting the ground to swallow me up. "I guess you could say that. So stop thinking you're old and past it."

"To be fair, you said *used to* have a crush, which suggests I got too old and hideous for you."

"Stop being such a needy bitch."

He laughed. "Sorry. I suppose I am being a bit needy but that was exactly the sort of ego-boost I needed today. So thanks for that."

"You're welcome."

Any fear I'd had of him being weirded out was immediately quashed. To be honest, I wasn't surprised. Gavin was an openminded dude and had always enjoyed being appreciated for his looks, regardless of who was doing the appreciating.

"Just out of interest," he said, "what was it about me that you liked?"

47

"Still fishing for compliments, are we?"

"I'm just curious. My spidey senses are telling me it's my cock that caught your interest."

"Your spidey senses don't know what they're talking about."

"Don't be embarrassed. You can admit it."

"When have I ever seen your dick, Gavin? When?"

He shrugged. "When I was taking a piss? We must have stood together at urinal at some point."

"We probably have but I can assure you I never made a point of looking. I would have been more focused on taking a piss myself."

"I wouldn't have cared if you did. Most men gauge the competition from time to time."

"Are you sure you're straight?"

"Quit avoiding the question," he said, mock-stern. "What was it about me that turned you on? And you can't say personality. No teenage boy jerks off over a personality."

He was right about that. But rather than tell him it was his sexy smell that had originally caught my attention, which sparked a perverted obsession with his armpits, which in turn fed a horny curiosity to want to lick them, I gave my stepfather a half-truth. "All of you. Face... body... I wasn't lying when I said you're a handsome dude."

A thoughtful look rippled across his face. "I am handsome, aren't I?"

"And incredibly modest."

He chuckled softly. "It's a shame you don't still have a thing for me."

"And why's that?"

"Because then I could bribe you to do my turn at the dishes in exchange for seeing more of this studly body of mine."

That earned him a flash of my middle finger.

He gave one right back, laughing some more. "If you did a really good job then I might even let you keep a pair of my dirty undies to keep under your pillow."

Gavin was just playing around and it was my turn to volley some piss-taking comment back, but words evaded me. My stepfather had no idea how close his joke was to describing some of my more shameful memories. Although I had never stored his underwear under my pillow, I had certainly taken a few guilty sniffs of his sweat-saturated undergarments in my younger days.

"What's wrong?" he asked, detecting my sudden awkwardness. "It was just a joke, Mikey."

"Yeah, I know. It just wasn't a very funny one."

"Anyway, buddy, thanks again for cheering me up. It almost makes up for me still wearing this cunting cock cage."

"You still have it on?"

"Yep."

"But why? Stryder cancelled."

"Fiona suggested I keep it on until we find someone else to have the threeway with."

"And you agreed?"

"It pays to keep her happy. And I'm sure I'll be rewarded for my sacrifice at some stage."

"Wouldn't she be happier if you could actually—"

"Use my cock?"

"Yeah."

"She has access to Gavin the Relentless, remember? The mould I made of my cock. So it ain't like my girl is going without."

I cringed.

"If you play your cards right," he continued, "then I could make you one for your birthday. Let you live out your Gav-the-man fantasy."

I barked a laugh, face burning, but fought to keep my tone aloof. "If you ever give me a dildo as a present then I'm telling you now it will end up as evidence in court as the weapon I used to murder you with."

"Is that your way of telling me you'd rather I give you the real thing?"

He kept smiling at me, and after a beat, my own mouth tipped up at the sides. We both started laughing, and for the first time today the vibe in the house felt like it was back to normal—even if it had taken a very abnormal conversation to get us there.

Chapter 5

IT MIGHT HAVE JUST been a dream but Brian looked fucking adorable. Messy hair all in the way of his glasses and lower lip caught between his teeth. We had just walked along a tropical beach, holding hands, telling each other how much we cared for one another. Now he was showing me how good he was at juggling by picking giant pieces of candy up out of the sand—five of them—and started throwing them around in the air.

I think that was the part where asleep me fully realised this wasn't real. It was also the part where asleep me decided to make the dream a bit wetter.

Whacking the juggled pieces of candy out of the way, I wrapped Brian up in my arms and forced him to kiss me. He hesitated. Dream Brian could be a fucker like that. But his hesitancy didn't stop me, and I slipped a hand down the front of his shorts, wrapping my fingers around his cock. It may have been a dream but what I felt beneath my fingers felt very real. It was hot, hard, and aching for me. So at odds with his protests: "Slow down, Mike. Let's talk a bit more."

"I don't want to talk. I want to fuck. I *need* to fuck."

My former best friend granted me my wish; kissing me back, and started thrusting his cock into the trap of my furled fingers.

He wasn't as big as I imagined the real Brian to be but that didn't matter. I was happy with whatever he had to offer.

A hideous beeping noise suddenly erupted from the clear blue sky around us and I could sense the dream coming to an end. The beach and ocean slowly disappeared and all that was left of the dream was Brian's moth on mine and his less than impressive cock in my hot little hand.

Our surroundings may have been gone but the beep was still there, like the most irritating echo I'd ever heard. Just as I thought I was about to feel Brian blast a sticky load into my hand, I woke up and discovered that the *less than impressive* cock I'd been touching was my own.

"Motherfucker," I muttered into my pillow.

Turning over, I saw the dream-wrecking culprit on my bedside table—my cell phone. It was flashing blue, letting me know I had messages.

After reaching over to grab my phone, I saw that they were from Jockey. Assuming it would be an update on his trip to visit his sick uncle, I was surprised when I opened it to see that he'd sent me two pictures of his sleepout.

The first photo was of the window near his bed. It had been smashed and there was glass all over the floor. The second picture showed his furniture—mattress, desk, bedside tables—trashed and tipped over on the floor. It looked like the Tasmanian Devil had stormed through his sleepout. Before I could respond to ask what had happened, a new message arrived, one without a picture.

Jockey: As predicted your whore took the bait. Have a nice day bitch.

I didn't have a clue what Jockey was on about. Wasn't he supposed to be on his way home from Kaitaia right now? After visiting a dying relative? Yet here he was sending me pictures of his trashed sleepout. Instinctively I knew better than to text back asking questions. Instead, I decided it was time to get up and make a start to my day.

I lifted the covers and glanced down at my cock. It had gone down a little but was still more hard than soft. I contemplated a quick wank before getting up, but thought better of it. It would be good practice to go without, I decided. After all, Jockey was expecting me to quit masturbating altogether once our contract came into effect. Such a demand seemed ridiculous but I figured it wouldn't be like I'd go without. Not with the amount of sex I was sure we would be having.

Rolling out of bed in just my boxers, I only managed to put on my socks before letting my grumbling tummy lead me in the direction of the kitchen in search of breakfast. With Jockey away, and Brian no longer a social option for geographical and fuckwit reasons, I had decided last night to spend the day working on my novel. Progress had been slow recently but each day saw the ending get a little closer.

As I passed the bathroom I saw steam emerging from under the door. I noticed that the door was partly open, and instinctively moved to shut it. As I did that though, I bumped against it and inadvertently pushed the door open even farther. I took a step inside, meaning to close it again. Over the sound of the shower running I heard Fiona's voice: "It takes practise but if you bother to give it a try I think you'll find you will enjoy it."

My first thought was: *But she didn't stay over last night.* And that's when I saw Gavin's phone on the stool near the shower. He was talking to her on speakerphone while he washed himself in the shower.

"Are you sure it will work?" he asked.

"That depends on you, baby. Every man is different. But you all have a magic button that if pressed *juuust right* can trigger amazing things."

Despite the tinniness of the phone's speaker, Fiona's voice had that distinctive purr of hers going on; the one she used when talking about something a bit flirty and dirty. That was enough to keep me rooted to the spot a little longer to hear what they were talking about.

Looking towards the shower, I saw that Gavin was visible through the sliding glass door. The glass was pebbled, and I didn't have a clear view, but his outline was visible and I saw enough that I was both embarrassed and transfixed.

"And you reckon it's a way for me to have an orgasm with this cage still on?" Gavin asked.

"If done right it will provide some relief. Maybe not in the way you're expecting but you'll feel good. Think of it as a bum cum."

"A bum cum," Gavin echoed. "I like the sound of that."

"Let's hope you like the feel of it too."

"Should I do it now while I'm in the shower?" Gavin asked.

"You can if you want but it would be best if you were laying down on the bed. That way you can use some lube to help ease your fingers in slowly."

OH MY FUCK!

They were talking about fingering! Gavin fingering his own asshole!

"But I'm horny now, baby," Gavin replied like a sullen child. "Me wanna bum cum."

"You're always horny," Fiona giggled. "That's what I love about you."

54

Gavin let out a frustrated growl, like a frisky tiger. "But I can do it in the shower, right?"

"It's up to you where you do it. But I do think you'd be better to do it in the bedroom with proper lubricant."

"I would but I don't want to risk Mike walking in."

"Tell him not to."

Gavin laughed. "It's not like I can say, 'sorry, buddy, but can you try not walking into my bedroom for a while, I'm about to go finger myself.'"

That annoyed me. I would never walk in his room without knocking. But then I guiltily reminded myself what I was doing right now—spying on him in a room that was also supposed to allow privacy.

Fiona chuckled. "Why not? Maybe Mike would like to join you?"

Gavin laughed before letting out another sexy growl. "You're such a dirty girl. I love it."

"Anyway, babe, I better get going," Fiona said, sounding like she was looking at a clock. "My Mum will be here soon to pick me and the kids up to go shopping. I'll see you this evening."

"Okay, sexy. I'll see you tonight." Gavin let out another tiger growl. "Wish me luck."

The shower door suddenly slipped open and it felt like my stomach dropped to my toes. I expected Gavin to step out naked and bust me standing there, spying. Thankfully all that came out from the steamy shower was a muscular brown arm as he reached over to switch off the call.

His arm disappeared back into the wet warmth of the shower. I watched as he bent his head back and let the water cascade down his body. His hands ran over his ass, and I glimpsed the dark outline of his crack for a moment as he wiped soap between his buttocks. I suddenly felt an ache in my groin. I reached down with my hand and found that I had stiffened in just the half a minute I'd been standing there.

My dick remained treacherously hard despite my attempts to will it down. *All you have to do is leave*, I told himself. *Just get the fuck out of here and shut the door!*

I tried to force myself to turn away, but my feet refused to move. Gavin, still oblivious, was continuing to wash his body. He bent over, running his hands up and down his hairy legs. Then he turned around and faced the showerhead.

First he let the spray hit him in the face, tilting his head back and letting it course down his neck. The glass and the steam prevented me from seeing him too clearly, and so I found myself pretending that it wasn't my stepfather I was watching but just some random dude.

Now that the bathroom was quiet I feared he would hear my breathing or even just sense another presence in the room. It would be difficult for him to see me, as the shower was tucked into the area behind the linen closet that was to my left. By standing across from the closet I could see around the corner, but Gavin would have to open the sliding pebbled-glass door to see me clearly.

The sound of the water hitting the tub floor filled my ears, and the steam that poured over the top of the shower door caressed my face. I had begun to sweat a little, and a bead trickled down my back. It was very hot, and underneath my boxers my body felt as if it were on fire. As if in a dream again I slipped a hand inside my boxers and wrapped my fingers around my hardness. I did nothing but hold it, feeling the blood beat beneath my fingers.

I saw the shadow of Gavin's hand reach up and touch the showerhead, making some kind of adjustment. The sound of the water changed from a gentle rain to something more forceful, and through the glass I saw that it now formed a single stream as it poured from the head. Gavin had taken a step back, and he now appeared to be hunched over facing away from the showerhead. One hand was pressed against the wall he was facing while the other reached back to explore his virgin ass.

I held my breath, imagining what might be happening behind the door. The jet from the shower angled down toward Gavin's moving hand, ending in a dull *tup-tup-tup* sound as his arm broke the force of its trajectory.

Gavin began to groan, just quietly, but loud enough I now knew for sure what he was doing in there. Pushing my boxers down, I released my erection. It sprang out full and aching into my palm. I stroked it slowly, my eyes fixed on the shower door where Gavin's fingerfucking show played out as if it were a dream. I felt my heartbeat accelerate to match the whirring of the showerhead, until the blood throbbed in my ears with the same sound: *Tup-tup-tup. Tup-tup-tup.*

I couldn't remember the last time a wank felt this good. As if by accident I'd become a voyeur hiding and watching, catching a man in his most private of moments. That the man was my stepfather didn't matter. I was excited beyond the point of being ashamed.

Gavin's moaning suddenly became more guttural and raw, almost beastlike. The groans grew in frequency and became a little louder with each plunge of his finger, each exploding from the steam like an explosion of fireworks: "Ahh-ahh-ahh." Gavin then used his other hand to punch the shower wall, cursing out. "Ough! Fucking hell!"

I felt a surging beneath my fingers and looked down just as a jet of cum erupted from my dick. The first blast fell to the floor, where it lay like a piece of string dropped onto the manky green carpet. The second and third jet I caught in my hand, the sticky wet heat filling my fingers. I forced myself to keep quiet, grinding my teeth as my body spasmed and my throat burned with the growls I was obliged to swallow unless I wanted to betray my presence to Gavin.

When my legs stopped shaking I quickly wiped my fouled hand on the inside of my boxers and pulled them up to cover my softening cock. The cum on the carpet I rubbed in with the toe of my sock. Then I opened the door and slipped outside, closing the door behind me just as the sound of the water ceased. I leaned my head against the door and heard the shower door slide open.

Gavin was muttering to himself: "If just one finger feels that bad I dread to think what a whole bloody cock would feel like."

I skedaddled towards the kitchen, desperate to put some distance between myself and the scene of a moral crime.

I avoided looking Gavin in the eye when he emerged from the bathroom, worried he could see guilt swirling in my pupils. It was an irrational fear but I promised myself to never let anything grow from the incident. Nothing had changed between us. He was still the same belching, farting, beer-drinking blue-collar bloke he'd always been. My stepfather. And yet, I couldn't stop sneaking glances at those handsome hands of his, wondering which finger had been given the honour.

Chapter 6

WE PULLED INTO THE long gravel drive and Gavin put the car in park. He was careful not to block the garage door. Fetching my phone from the console, I glanced at the time as I unlocked the screen. I didn't have work today so I had agreed to come with Gavin to visit his best mate Trent. The invite had been given over breakfast this morning, mere minutes after spying on him in the shower. Gavin had been unusually keen for me to accompany him, insisting we were overdue a day of hanging out together. Normally I would have turned down the invite but, fuelled by guilt of what I'd done, I'd agreed to come with him.

I sent Jockey a text asking how his visit to Kaitaia was going before getting out of the car and stretching. The sun was climbing in the Sunday morning sky and my decision to wear a singlet already felt like the right choice.

Following a few feet behind Gavin, we passed by Trent's white work van. **Pembroke Builders** was emblazoned across the side. Much like the man himself the business name was short and basic. As we made our way toward the front porch, I glanced at the 1970s four-bedroom home sat atop a concrete basement, amazed at how nice Trent and Donna had made the place. It probably helped that the married couple did alright for themselves financially. Donna worked parttime at a call centre and Trent's one-man building business earned them enough to make sure they lived pretty good for a family of seven.

We climbed the brick steps to find the door already opening in front of us. Trent stood in the doorway, smiling like a man who had just won the lottery. Smooth-faced and with product in his mousy brown hair—that I suspect he'd dyed recently—he actually resembled the young athlete with wet-spiked hair of his youth. He was also dressed smartly in beige chinos and a black collar-shirt that did an amazing job of slimming down his beer belly.

"Hey...," Trent's cherry greeting got lost to a questioning sneer. "Why isn't Fiona with you?"

"Change of plans," Gavin said. "So I brought Mike along instead."

I couldn't see Gavin's face but based on the small nod Trent gave him I assumed Gavin had just mouthed something to him.

After regarding me with a cool smile, Trent sighed and said, "Come on in, fellas."

We stepped into the living room of Trent's house, careful to take our shoes off at the door. It was the tidiest I had ever seen the house, not a single kids' toy in sight. The silence in the house told me that all five children must have been out with Donna.

Out the corner of my eye I saw Trent give me another frosty look. "I'm just going to go get changed," he said. "Be back in a jiffy."

When Trent disappeared into the hallway, I turned to Gavin and whispered, "Does Trent have a problem with me being here?"

"No. Why?"

"Well, he keeps looking at me like I'm some bad smell you've dragged in off the street."

"Don't worry about that. He'll get over it."

"Get over what?"

Gavin flashed me a smile dipped in guilt sauce. "It doesn't matter."

"Just tell me," I whisper-shouted. "I don't want to be somewhere I'm not wanted."

"Trent was expecting me and Fiona here today for the Die-Hard movie marathon." He lowered his voice to add, "You catch my drift?"

I caught his drift. Fiona had promised Gavin that if he pushed his sexual boundaries by agreeing to have sex with another man then she would reward him with a sexual fantasy of his own. And Gavin's fantasy was a Die-Hard movie marathon with his best mate while Fiona spent the day sucking them both off.

"No wonder he doesn't want me here," I said.

"You're fine."

"Why didn't you tell him sooner the whole Die-Hard thing wasn't happening?"

"Because I know how much he's been looking forward to it and...." His words got lot to another guilty smile.

"And?"

"And I thought if I broke the news to him while you're here then he won't get so shitty."

That explained why Gavin had been so keen for me to join him. Fucker.

"You should have just told him over the phone," I said. "I'm sure he'd understand."

Gavin scoffed. "We're talking about a man who hasn't had a blowjob since high school. He's been looking forward to this even more than I have."

I should have been more weirded out by Gavin assisting his best mate to commit adultery, but if the past few weeks had taught me anything it was that I could become desensitized to the weird and immoral.

Gavin opened his mouth to speak but no words came out when he became distracted by something behind me.

"Shall we go down to the mancave?"

I turned around and saw Trent standing in the doorway of the hallway. He had gotten changed into his usual attire of baggy t-shirt and equally baggy basketball shorts. I suppose he wore such clothes for comfort but they didn't flatter his physique. If anything they made the short thirty-something look podgier than he actually was.

We followed Trent and descended the carpeted steps to the basement AKA the mancave. The basement was Trent's pride and joy, and probably the only part of the house he held domain over and got any peace and quiet.

On one side of the room was an old threadbare rug covering the concrete floor near a huge flatscreen television, and two old armchairs and a chrome table with a yellow formica top. There was also an old red velvet sofa, the kind that makes one feel itchy just looking at it. Papering the cinder-block walls were posters of rock groups and scantily-clad bikini models. The other half of the spacious room was what Trent referred to as the 'fun zone'. Yeah, the guy was a big kid at heart. The fun zone housed an old pinball machine, ping-pong and pool tables, a punching bag, a rack of free-weights and a half-finished bar in one dusty, forgotten corner. The bar had been a pet project that Trent had worked on years ago but he'd either run out of money or lost interest before finishing it.

Instead, an old Kelvinator refrigerator painted blue played the role of drink station.

I glanced over at the television and saw that the first Die Hard movie was loaded onto the screen, just waiting for someone to press play. There was a plush red cushion on the floor in front of the couch—which I assumed was so Fiona didn't get sore knees.

Gavin wasted no time fetching a pool stick from the wall. Trent didn't immediately join him. He walked over and found the remote to the TV and switched it off. He then went and grabbed another pool cue from the wall.

"Any beer in the fridge?" Gavin asked.

"Mate, it's not even nine yet," he said.

Gavin smirked. "Not really seeing your point."

With a smile, Trent went and fetched us each a beer from the fridge while Gavin began racking the balls on the table. Whatever frosty mood had possessed Trent at the front door seemed to have melted away.

"Trent and I will play the first round," Gavin said. "Winner will play Mike. Then the winner of that will play whoever lost the first match and so on and so on."

"Sounds good to me," Trent said.

I excused myself to go upstairs and use the bathroom and let them get the first game under way. After taking a quick piss, I washed my hands and was about to make my way back downstairs when I heard Gavin's voice coming from the kitchen.

"It's not my fault. It really was supposed to be happening."

"Are you sure?" Trent's voice replied. "Because right now I'm starting to think this has been one big joke at my expense."

I walked towards the kitchen where they were talking, wondering why they hadn't stayed downstairs to start their game.

There was no one there. *But I'm sure this is where the voice was coming from.* For a split-second I thought Trent's house must have been haunted but then I heard Gavin's voice coming from the bench near the electric kettle.

"Why on earth would I make up a story about letting a guy fuck my ass just so we can both get a blowie from my missus? If anything the joke is on me."

It wasn't ghosts impersonating my stepfather and his best mate it was an old baby monitor set up beside the electric jug. I would have spent some time questioning why the hell a baby monitor was set up here and down in the basement but the conversation I was hearing was too engrossing.

"I'm sorry, Gav," Trent said. "It's just that I was really looking forward to it."

"I know, mate. Me too. I can't take this fucking cock cage off until it happens."

Trent laughed. "You're a braver man than me. I couldn't go that long without playing with myself."

"Tell me about it. I was so desperate this morning that I even tried giving myself a bum cum."

"A what?" Trent asked.

"A bum cum. Fiona told me if I finger my ass just the right way that I could give myself a prostate massage and maybe get off that way."

Another laugh from Trent. "And how did it go?"

"Not well. I got two in up to the knuckle, pushed a bit too hard and hurt myself. So no bum cum. Just two stinky fingers."

They started laughing and the monitor went fuzzy for a moment. When the sound returned I heard Gavin speaking again:

"I promise it will happen. It's just gonna take a little longer than expected."

"Maybe we should forget about it," Trent said. "We're not the silly teenagers we were when we made that Die-Hard promise."

"Don't be like that, mate. I gave you my word and I intend on coming through. Fiona just needs to set me up with a bloke who isn't gonna chicken out at the last minute."

The monitor went quiet for a lingering moment until finally Trent's quiet voice spoke. "What if I did it?"

"Did what?" Gavin asked.

"You know...hook up with you." Trent sounded like he was blushing. "It might be easier if you do it with someone you know. We used to kiss all the time when we got drunk at parties."

"I appreciate the offer, but Fiona doesn't wanna just see me kiss another bloke, she wants me to go all the way."

"What if I gave you a handjob? Would that count? We watched each other jerk off enough while growing up, so I'm pretty sure I know how you like it."

This was news to me. I'd heard the stories of them kissing many times but never once had mutual masturbation been mentioned.

Gavin laughed. "I wish it were that simple."

"Bugger."

"Bugger indeed," Gavin quipped.

The next thing I heard was the satisfying *clunk* of one of them lining up to take his shot to break the set of pool balls.

Trent's voice: "I hope you know that I don't expect you to go through with this just to make me happy. Just because me and Donna are divorcing doesn't mean you have to throw a pity suck my way."

Trent and Donna are divorcing!? That was something else that was news to me. Now it made a little more sense why Gavin hadn't seem bothered about helping his best mate commit adultery.

"As much as I love ya, mate," Gavin replied, "it's not you I'm doing it for. I want an all-day suckjob as much as you do. The fact you benefit from it is just a bonus."

Gavin said something I couldn't quite make out and then it went quiet between them again.

Then: "What are your plans for tomorrow night?" Trent asked.

"Nothing planned as of yet."

"What do you say to bringing Fiona round so we can watch the Die-Hard films together? At least just one of them."

"Doesn't that defeat the purpose?"

"Not necessarily," Trent said, sounding like an undercover agent. "Donna and the kids don't get back from her mother's until Friday so we'd still have the place to ourselves."

"And?"

"*And* maybe if Fiona sees the trouble I've gone to in setting up the movie night that she might just give you your fantasy anyway."

"You've rented the Die-Hard franchise, Trent, not built a castle."

"I've done more than that," Trent said defensively. "I've also bought a bottle of top shelf whiskey for the occasion. And there's cheese platters made up in the fridge. Fancy shit like brie and camembert."

"I'm sorry, mate, but you're clutching at straws. Fiona ain't going anywhere near your dick until she's sees me sit on one."

"What if you asked her for a compromise?"

"What sort of compromise?"

"Ask her to let your little fella out of the cage and I can sit and watch her suck you off."

"Really?" I could hear the frown in Gavin's voice. "You'd be keen for just that? Some voyeur shit?"

"It's better than the alternative."

"Which is?"

"Me sat down here rubbing one out to the same boring shit on Pornhub every night."

My stepfather must have been giving it some serious thought because he was taking a long time to respond. "What if—"

Gavin's response was cut off by an almighty sneeze. A sneeze coming from me!

"What the fuck was that?" said Gavin.

Uh oh...

A shiver chilled down my spine.

"Oopsy daisy," Trent said in an adorably dopey voice. "I forgot that was on."

"Why the hell have you got a bloody baby monitor down here?" Gavin asked.

"Donna uses it so she doesn't have to walk down here to tell me when dinner is ready."

Gavin let out a frustrated sigh and I imagined him slapping a palm to his face. He then very calmly said, "Are you coming back down to play pool, Mike? Or would you rather stay up there eavesdropping?"

With a face bright enough to replicate Rudolph the Reindeer's nose, I returned to the basement for the most awkward game of pool in my life.

Chapter 7

THANKFULLY GAVIN AND Trent didn't say anything about me eavesdropping. We just played pool, had a couple beers, and pretended like the whole thing never happened. But that all changed the moment Gavin and I hopped in the car to go home just before lunchtime.

"Did you enjoy listening to mine and Trent's *private* conversation?" Gavin asked as soon as he started the engine.

With a face full of cringe, I began to ramble out an apology. "I'm so sorry about that. I shouldn't have been eavesdropping. But once I started listening I guess I got hooked and—"

"Don't sweat it," Gavin replied with a laugh. "You didn't hear anything I wouldn't tell you to your face."

"If that's the case how come you never told me about Trent and Donna getting a divorce?"

"Oh yeah. I forgot about that part. But now you know." He turned to me and added, "Probably best you pretend you never heard that. Donna will kill him if it gets around town."

"Why does it have to be a secret if they've already decided to break up?"

"Donna is from good old catholic stock and she doesn't want to go public with the split until she's ready."

"And Trent is happy to go along with that?"

"If it delays him having to pay child support then I don't think Trent minds so much. All he's worried about is the lack of nookie. But I gather that's been a problem for a while."

"It must be worrying him a lot if he's resorting to offering you a handjob."

Gavin nodded. "Tell me about it. I certainly wasn't expecting that."

"Just like I wasn't expecting to hear how you two used to watch each other masturbate."

Gavin's shoulders shook with silent laughter. "Very funny, smart ass. You know what boys are like growing up. One minute you're playing truth or dare and the next minute you've both got your pants down to see who can squirt the most."

"And how often did you and Trent like to play this game?" It was meant as a joke but sounded more like a genuine question.

"I dunno. Quite a lot. It wasn't really a game after a while. Just something different to do when we'd knock about after school." Gavin chuckled to himself. "Trent would steal his father's nudie mags and we'd go down to the woodshed and look at the pictures together."

That's quite the close friendship, I thought, but decided not to probe.

"Shit like that is totally normal," Gavin said, more for his benefit than mine. "All those hormones buzzing about in your body. Makes you crazy. And in boys it brings out a competitive streak. Almost like it's an excuse to see whose got a bigger cock."

I choked down a dry swallow. "Who was bigger?"

"Wouldn't you like to know," Gavin said smugly.

That's why I asked, dick.

"What about you?" Gavin looked over at me. "You and your mates must have some funny stories."

"In my day we just played videogames," I said in a faux-posh accent.

"Bullshit. You can't tell me you and Brian never goofed about like that growing up. It's what mates do."

Is it? "Well, we didn't."

"Really?" Gavin raised an eyebrow at me. "What boring little sods."

I know it was just a joke but it was a joke that stabbed my fragile ego. Without thinking I blurted, "Jockey used to suck me off on Friday nights for fun."

Gavin's eyebrows arched. "You win," he said.

"I didn't realise it was a competition."

"It wasn't," he said sincerely.

As we rode along in silence, I began to psychoanalyse why I had shared such an inappropriate memory with my stepfather. Was I trying to impress him? Or was it my way of taking a potshot at Jockey? I suspected it was the latter on account of how I purposely left out that it was now me who was the cocksucker in the friendship.

Gavin finally broke the silence. "Fiona told me Jockey was a bit partial to that sort of thing, but I thought it was just her way of trying to get me to agree to a threesome."

"I wouldn't know."

"You just said he used to polish your knob, so I'd say you know better than anyone." He turned his face, smiling. "Are there any other juicy Jockey stories you can tell me?"

"Why are you so interested in whatever Jockey's done?"

"It just pays to know a bit about the competition. And a girlfriend's ex is *always* competition."

"I can't think of any other stories," I lied.

"Are you sure? A bj is pretty out there."

"I wouldn't say that." My voice sounded tense. "You just said yourself it's the sort of thing mates do while growing up. Just dumb boy stuff."

"I wish my dumb boy stuff had been that adventurous. If Trent had let me practise on his mouth then I wouldn't have lost my lollies in ten seconds the first time a girl went down on me."

"So you and Trent never touched each other?"

"Never." Gavin shook his head. "We just jerked off in front of each other. Until we got older, of course, and would make out at parties for a laugh."

"Okay."

"I think we were too worried that if we touched, like that, that it would make us something we weren't. Stupid really, since I'm sure we were both curious at the time what the other felt like."

"Felt like?"

"Our dicks," Gavin said bluntly. "I can't speak for Trent but I would have been game to give him a tug. Just to know what another bloke's tool felt like."

Was Gavin talking like this on purpose? Trying to get a rise out of me? Well, it was working in one respect because against my wishes, my dick began to get hard.

"I think that's why I'm so cool with what Fiona's been asking me to do," Gavin said. "It will give me a chance to be brave again. But this time have the guts to go through with it."

"Then why don't you just ask Trent? He sounds hard up enough to accept a handjob."

71

Gavin laughed. "I'm not saying I want to get hot and heavy with that hairy critter. Bless him. What I'm saying is that life gives us opportunities to explore things and be brave. Trent and I had that opportunity at sixteen, but we missed it. Sometimes though, if we're lucky, life presents new opportunities. And we should seize them with both hands and learn from them."

Gavin's bizarre spiel left me feeling uncomfortable, so I responded the only way I knew how. With humour. "It would have to be a pretty big dick to seize it with both hands."

"I think you know I'm not just talking about cocks, Mike. I'm talking about anything. New job. Travelling overseas. Anything that might be an adventure. I'm old enough now that it pays to say yes to these things. No matter what others might think of you."

I nodded, sensing there was more to Gavin's speech than he was letting on.

"Sometimes the right moment, or person, is right under our noses and we don't even realise it," he continued. "Someone that others might say isn't right for you but you know that their wrong. That you and this person have a fire. A spark. Chemistry."

There was a twinkle in Gavin's eye. A secret. Something special he wanted to share with me.

Still smiling, Gavin said, "Yesterday a certain someone told me something that I can't stop smiling about. In fact, I woke up this morning yahooing just thinking about it. All I have thought about today is how I want to ask this person something that will put a smile on their face too. But I'm worried how they'll react."

Oh my God!

Gavin was talking about me! Talking about how I had confessed to having a crush on him when I was younger. I felt dizzy. Speechless. Which was a shame because I wanted to tell him to just come out and say it. It all made sense now. All this talk about same-sex attraction, and how he wanted to explore that side of himself. It wasn't so he could find out if he had a bi side, it was so he could finally act on these feelings.

Heat was definitely rising between my legs. And in my heart. I suddenly realised that I had never stopped having a crush on this man. Not really. I had only ever buried it because it had felt like the right thing to do. How could I not be into Gavin? He was a total stud with a heart of gold. That sexual tension between us suddenly felt like the flame of a lit match to pure oxygen. Only it felt stronger, nuclear, the Big Bang that started all life in the universe.

"I know what you're talking about," I said, smiling just as much as Gavin. "And I think you should totally ask this person that question."

"You think?"

"Absolutely. I'm pretty sure their smile will be just as big as yours."

Gavin let out a deep breath. "Oh, Mike. You don't know how good it feels to hear you say that. I was worried how you'd react."

"Really? I thought you'd know I'd be totally on board for this."

Gavin shook his head. "I can't say I did."

"Well, I am on board. So now all you have to do is get that key so you can unlock that big dick of yours."

He laughed. "Who said it was big?"

"You did. More than once."

"Maybe I've been fibbing." He shot me a flirty wink. "It might just be a little brown saveloy for all you know."

"I guess I'll find out when the cage comes off."

73

He gave me a weird look, almost scrutinizing, then returned his attention to the road. "Knowing Fiona she will want me to keep the cage on until the wedding night."

The wedding night!?

"You know," Gavin said, "it wasn't until she called me last night to tell me she loved me that I even realised I wanted to marry her."

Chapter 8

WEDNESDAY MORNING THE weather was overcast, and I knew it would rain before the day was done. I'd had a bowl of cereal for breakfast that tasted like sawdust soaked with milk and left the house without a jacket or umbrella. Gavin was still in bed when I snuck outside. He was making the most of sleeping in on a weekday. Following his Fiona epiphany over the weekend, my stepfather had decided to take the week off work so he could in his words "wine and dine my baby every night and then surprise her on Sunday with an engagement ring."

It must have been love, I decided, because Gavin had never been one to splurge on the women he dated. But every night this week he'd taken Fiona out for dinner, bought her bottles of wine that weren't picked up from a bargain barrel, and would bring her home to the house and rub her feet on the couch before bed. I'd never seen the man so pussy-whipped. Gavin was usually much more prudent with his finances, but I preferred what my mother used to say whenever they'd fight about money: *Gavin Masters, you are tighter than a snapper's asshole!*

Unfortunately for me it wasn't the tightness of his wallet I couldn't stop thinking about. I wanted to jam my cock into my stepfather, so hard that he'd never forget me, so that he'd touch his handsome ass twenty years from now and think of me and howl, but...

It was never going to happen.

Which is why for the past three days any chance I could get I would get out of the house and put some distance—both physically and emotionally—between us. It was as if an old wound had been cut open and now my guts was hanging out. That was the best way to describe my reignited crush on Gavin. For years it had remained dormant inside my heart, deep enough I wasn't even aware of its existence, but after stupidly thinking he had feelings for me there was nothing I could do to hide from my attraction to the man.

I still couldn't believe that I had stupidly thought he could be in to me. How mental was I? Seriously, what idiot thinks his pussy-mad stepfather wants to shag him? This idiot apparently. To be fair, I felt like I had every reason to question his sexuality because of the threesome he had planned. But the harsh truth was that had nothing to do with any secret yearning Gavin may have had for cock, but everything to do with trying to impress the kinky big-titted blonde he hoped to call his wife.

When I reached the corner shops, I stopped and bought myself a fizzy drink then carried on in the direction of Hickford Park. That should have been the last place I would be headed but right now it felt like the safest place to be alone with my thoughts. Besides, it wasn't as if I would run into any trouble there at this time of the day.

Trouble seems to find me though.

Although that thought was my own I couldn't help but feel that maybe it was my way of playing the victim to excuse some responsibility. I was the one who fancied Gavin. I was the one who had signed Jockey's contract. And I was the one who'd foolishly allowed myself to be christened a Hickford Homo.

Maybe that's why I was headed to that park. It was a part of me and my story now. I had fallen victim to my own lust and would forever be connected to all the me who'd found themselves with that label. Thankfully the only people who knew my secret shame were Jockey and Damian. And there was no way Damian would be spilling that gossip unless he fancied others in town knowing he too had been tarred with the same brush for years now. My former babysitter also had to be mindful people didn't find out how he supplemented his benefit income with his trips to the park.

At least I haven't sunk that low.

I held onto that thought as if it were a life raft. Cruel as it was, I felt better to have someone else to look down on. But beneath the surface, buried under what was left of my pride, I knew that I was every bit as damaged as Damian Takarangi was.

AS I HAD SUSPECTED, Hickford Park was empty when I got there. It wasn't even ten o'clock yet, so it was still too early for the teenage delinquents to hang out smoking cigarettes and pot. I went and sat on a faded park bench beneath an old oak tree, and admired the scraggly patch of greenery with its industrial surroundings. In the distance, across the field, I could see the small forested hill that was home to the pigpen and the site of my corruption at the hands of my former babysitter.

Fishing my phone out of my pocket, I began to scroll through Instagram. Not being able to stalk Brian anymore took a lot of the fun out of it, but I entertained myself with strangers thirst traps and pictures of celebrities flaunting their wonderful lives. Eventually I grew tired of admiring those I did not know, so I went to Damian's page to see what he had on offer.

To my surprise, Damian had uploaded a whole bunch of pics last night from some piss-up he'd been at. Most of the pictures were of him and a bunch of other guys drinking around a bonfire. They were a rough-looking bunch with their scowls and face and neck tattoos. I recognised a few of them from the neighbourhood. They were the sorts of guys that Gavin would tell me to stay clear of. Once upon a time they would have been the sort of guys Damian would have stayed clear of too, but I guess these days he just went wherever he could score something to get high.

My eyebrows climbed in surprise when I swiped to a video that showed a shirtless Damian with his tongue down the throat of some skinny ginger chick. The pair looked equally wasted; sluggish limbs, sloppy mouths. When they'd finished pashing, Damian turned to the camera, his arm around the girl, as if to say: *I'm the man*.

Someone off screen yelled, "Take her inside and give her one, bro."

Damian responded with a smug tilt of the head as he gave one of the girl's tits a grope. They then locked mouths again, playing it up for the camera.

I wondered how the other guys cheering Damian on would react if they knew what he did to afford the drugs he bought from them. And I wondered how the girl would react if she knew her tongue was inside the mouth of a man who only days ago was drinking piss straight from another dude's dick.

"Whatcha doing, bitch?"

The voice startled me. I turned to see Jockey coming towards me, a cocky strut in his stride. He was wearing cargo shorts that showed off his shaggy calves, short work boots that had seen better days, and a form-fitting white singlet that emphasised the lines of his tasty torso and gave me a great view of brown chest hair curling over the top.

About to ask how he knew where to find me, I remembered the tracing app he'd put on my phone. I greeted him with a smile and put my phone away.

He returned an even brighter smile. "You do know your people, the Hickford Homos, don't come out to play until it gets dark, right?"

"I just came here to chill out."

"I know. I'm just teasing." But he looked me up and down, eyes moving slow over my body, as if to assess if I was, in fact, here to chill out.

"How come you're not at work?" I asked.

"I don't start till twelve today."

"Okay."

"Anyway, I came to tell you the good news. I just got a message from the clinic. Your results are in and you're clean as a whistle."

"That's good."

"You don't sound excited? You should be happy."

"I am happy. I'm just...just tired." I tried to inject some enthusiasm into my voice when I asked my next question. "Does this mean we can start the contract today?"

"I was thinking it might be best if we wait until Monday."

"Oh..."

"What's *oh*?"

"Are you having second thoughts about this?" I asked.

"No. What makes you think that?"

"Well...you keep putting it off."

"Don't let that fool you. I'm excited as fuck for you to become mine. Every day since you signed your name to the contract I've been rubbing one out while thinking about all the sexy shit I'm gonna do with you."

"Yeah?"

Grinning like he had canary feathers stuck in his teeth, Jockey said, "It's a big *yeah*."

"So, um, why are we waiting for Monday if you're that excited?"

"Because I need to sort out some other matters first. Then I can then focus on being the best alpha to my faggot that I can." He gave my thigh a gentle squeeze. "Your pussy will thank me for it later."

I laughed softly. "I'm sure my pussy will."

"But remember, I want you to behave yourself until then. If you screw around then make sure you wear a rubber. At least until you've been on those pills for seven days."

Screwing around was the furthest thing from my mind but I nodded anyway. "Deal," I said, holding out my hand.

"I don't shake hands with faggots," he said with a sneer. "No offense."

How could I not be offended? But I knew better than to verbalise that thought.

"And remember," Jockey said, "I want you to bring me the condom afterwards. Just to show me you know how to play safe."

"Riight." There was more than an ounce of sarcasm in my voice.

Jockey's obsession with me bringing him a used rubber was odd, I thought. I was pretty sure it had less to do with me playing safe than for him to find a way to exert some authority and control.

Jockey reached into the pockets of his shorts and pulled out a small white envelope that had my name written on it. "This is for you," he said. "It has some permission slips for you to use. Remember the blue ones I showed you?"

Of course I remembered. How could I forget? Blue forms were what I needed to use if I wanted Jockey's permission to sleep with another man, and yellow forms were orders telling me the name of a man he *expected* me to sleep with.

"Now technically you don't need to start using them until Monday," Jockey explained, "but I was thinking if you do choose to skank your pussy about before then it would be good if you used them. Just so I can keep track of the sorts of men you've been with. There's also a wee note in there for you to read."

My fingers were quick to open the envelope but he stopped me. "Not right now," he said, closing his hand over mine. "You can read it later."

I slipped the envelope into my pocket.

"Scoot closer," Jockey said.

I slid closer to him on the rough bench, and he surprised me by putting his arm around me and drew me up against his bony shoulder. I tentatively lay my head on it. He smelled strongly of sweat and under that, faintly of sawdust. The position felt strange, almost alien, weirdly tender. But still, I felt the menace in his sinewy muscles and heard the dominance in his voice when he next spoke.

"Unzip your pants. I wanna play with your dick."

"What? Right here?"

"Yes right here. Ain't no one around to see."

A quick glance around the park confirmed he was correct. Still, I wasn't overly keen on exposing myself in a public space during daylight hours.

"You're safe with me, Mike," he said, the command in his voice snagging me out of my whirling thoughts. "Now unzip your pants."

I gracelessly unzipped my jeans and rooted around inside. A moment later, my cock—timid, shy, but slowly stiffening—was out of my jeans and in Jockey's hand.

My face burned. A different kind of heat burned between my legs.

"I love how small you are," he said, playing with my dick like it was no big deal. "It's such a cute little dicky."

If his intention was to make me feel small and self-conscious then he was succeeding, not that my dick had a problem with any of it. The more Jockey touched my penis the more it swelled between his fingers, and pretty soon I was fully erect. The part of me that wanted to stay in control, mentally begged him to stop. That part of me didn't like or appreciate what was happening. It still could not accept the embarrassing truth: I enjoyed—no, got off on—being used and humiliated.

Icy-hot shivers cycloned through my body. His thumb swirled around my piss slit, casual like, as if he were twirling the tip of a pen. I kept waiting for him to give another order, something that would take this molestation into deeper sexual territory, but that order never came. It was only when he began to tell me about the building site he'd be working on today that I realised this was all he wanted—me beside him with my cock in his hand. More than once he got me close to climax but each time he would let go, warned by the pitch of my breath, and then wait for me to soften a little before grabbing my cock again.

When he had finished telling me about the worksite, a thick silence settled over us and my paranoia of someone catching us returned. There still didn't appear to be anyone around but that didn't mean someone wouldn't pass by soon. I raised my head from his shoulder and gently tried to slide away, hoping he'd get the message I was uncomfortable, but it only served to make him grip my *little dicky* tighter.

Accepting the fact my dick was a prisoner of his fingers until he said otherwise, I asked, "How was your Uncle Ralph?"

"Who?"

"Ralph," I said. "Your sick relative you went to visit in Thames."

"Oh, Ralph." Jockey chuckled. "I've no idea."

"What?" I gasped suddenly when he gave my cock a firm tug. "I-I thought you went to visit him?"

"Nope." Jockey smiled as he swivelled a finger over the precum forming on my tip. "I didn't go see him because he ain't real."

"Come again?"

His eyebrows climbed as if to say *Are you an idiot?* "You didn't think that was true, did you?"

"Uh..." Shit, it was hard to concentrate when I was so close to blowing a load. "But you said—"

"None of that shit was real. The sick uncle. The drugs. It was all a ploy to trick Damian. What do you think the picture of the broken window was about? That was to show you that your whore took the bait. It was all part of the plan."

I had been so consumed about my Gavin problem that I'd totally forgotten about Jockey sending me those pictures. But even so, I'd had no way of knowing that broken window had anything to do with Damian. Either Jockey hadn't realised he'd forgotten to tell me the finer details of his plan, or he assumed I was a mind reader. Although I was still confused, and borderline delirious from this constant edging going on between my thighs, I was mostly relieved to know the drugs hadn't been real. The last thing I needed was to have my ass owed by a drug dealer.

Jockey began to explain in detail about how he'd set Damian up. The arrangement where he Damian would be paid to have sex with me was the first part of the plan so Jockey could then dangle the bait. And the bait of course had been all the drugs and the cash. However, the drugs were fake. The money, although real, had been put straight back in his wallet after Damian and I had left. Even asking Damian to drink his piss had been part of the plan—sort of.

"Don't get me wrong," Jockey said. "I got him to do that because I enjoyed it, and you did need some pointers since I will expect you to drink me at some point, but it was mostly to see just how far Damian was willing to go in the hope of getting his hands on those drugs. Once he'd done that, drank my piss for nothing, I knew for sure I could count on the cunt breaking in. Shit, if he didn't do it just for the drugs then he would have done it just to get back at me. That's when I told you both about dear old uncle Ralph."

Jockey then went into detail about how later that night he had sat alone in the dark of his sleepout waiting for my former babysitter to return. Apparently he didn't have to wait that long. Just before 10 pm Damian smashed a window to get in before raiding the drawers to find the drugs and the money. When the drug addict couldn't find what he was looking for he began to throw shit around in a fit of anger while trying to find where they might be. It was only when Damian bothered to go look in the bathroom that he found a smiling Jockey hidden behind the partially opened door and recording the whole break-in on his phone.

"Did he get violet?" I asked?"

"Nope. The pussy got such a fright he just turn and ran."

"But if the drugs weren't"—my voice got lost to another soft moan from the heavenly feel of his fingers— "weren't real, then what was the stuff in the bag you showed us?"

"Mash potato flakes."

"Mash potato flakes? Are you serious?"

"Yep." Jockey laughed. "The idiot broke in to steal something that all he could do with was add water to. Dumb cunt."

To be fair to Damian, I'd also assumed the white substance in the bag was drugs. And to be fair to both of us, Jockey had only dangled the bag in the air for a few seconds before promptly putting it back in the drawer.

"So what exactly did tricking Damian achieve?" I asked. "Aside from him smashing your window."

"It means I've got him by the balls. That thieving prick knows as well as I do that if he gets done for burglary again then his ass will go inside again, and not just for six months this time. He'll get at least four years."

"I don't want him to go to jail. Not when he's been set him up like that."

"Why are you being so soft? That asshole beat you and robbed you. Prison is the least he deserves."

"Is it though?" I mashed my lips together, silencing another groan.

Before answering, Jockey took a squizz at my cock, admiring the sticky fluid I was leaking all over his fingers. "Don't stress it.

As much as he deserves a holiday behind bars Damian won't go to jail...if he's smart."

"Meaning?"

"Meaning he either signs a contract to become my faggot or I'll send the video to the pigs."

"But you already have a...*me*."

My heart was beating fast, and my chest was constricting, and I knew it had nothing to do with the expert handjob I was receiving. I wasn't normally a jealous person, but the feeling expanding in my chest couldn't be anything else. The idea of Damian becoming Jockey's faggot made me want to destroy shit.

"Don't get all jelly on me," Jockey said, picking up what I was feeling. "You're still gonna be my number one. Besides, I might not even keep him for the duration of the contract. I was thinking I could just loan him out to a mate in exchange for some cash."

"You have mates who would pay for Damian?"

"I'm looking at one right now." Jockey smirked and reached into my fly to give my balls a tickle.

"You know what I mean," I snapped, sounding angrier than I intended.

Ignoring my comment, Jockey drew my balls out from the warmth of my jeans so they could join my cock in the cool morning air. "Your balls could do with another shave." He rubbed over the hairs sprouting up from my scrotum. "Make sure you clean that up before Monday. I expect my faggot to have smooth nads."

"Yes, sir."

He grabbed hold of my cock again and resumed pumping me. "And in answer to your question, I know of a few guys who might be interested in buying Damian. Dudes I've connected with online in the local area. There's a lot of alphas out there keen for a faggot to call their own. There just ain't many fags like you in a town like this who will sign a contract to become another man's possession. That's part of the reason I was so fucking stoked you signed it. The other alphas will think I'm the man."

That sounded like the Jockey I knew. Not the master, or the sex fiend, but the misunderstood outcast desperately seeking approval wherever could get it.

Gripped by another pleasant shiver, I replied with chattering teeth, "Th-There's no way Damian will sign the contract. H-He's too stubborn for that."

"I wouldn't be so sure about that. I spoke to him yesterday about it and showed him the video."

"And?"

"And he told me to go fuck myself." Jockey laughed. "The fucker even took a swing at me."

"That's your answer right there."

Jockey shook his head. "Nar. When he calmed down he asked me if he could have a few days to think it over. Do a bit of soul searching. That tells me he is going to sign it."

I thought about the pictures I'd just seen on Damian's Instagram. It didn't look like he was doing much *soul searching* about Jockey's ultimatum. "Or he's buying time to do a runner," I said.

"Maybe. But he'd be stupid if he did. The pigs would end up finding him and he'd go away for even longer."

He'd also be stupid to sign the contract, I thought privately.

Chuckling to himself, Jockey then said, "I can't believe you thought I was dealing."

"In my defence, you have surprised me in many ways these past few weeks. Adding drug dealer to the list seemed just another new thing."

"I only smoke pot. And cigarettes." He lowered his voice. "And your ass when it's on the end of my dick."

Jockey's wrist suddenly began to pick up the pace, so too did my noise level increase: hard breathing, grunts, gasps, and groans. Had anybody been walking nearby they would've heard me, but at that moment I didn't care.

"You like that do you, bitch?"

"You know I do. You know I—" My balls tingled, my legs clenched. "Coming! I'm coming! I'm—" My words got lost to a moan as an almighty climax gripped my body.

Still jerking me, Jockey placed his other hand directly in front of my cock, milliseconds before my load exploded and I squirted twice—*tthhit-tthhhit*—into the palm of his hand.

My breathing began to slow down while Jockey milked my cock of all its remaining drops. When he was sure there was no more juice to drain, he pulled his hand up to his face and took a whiff of my seed. Then, sexy as fuck, my man licked up the thick pool of cum in his hand, slurping noisily to let me know just how much he enjoyed my taste.

Smiling, Jockey said, "I think that's breakfast taken care of." And then he walked off just as abruptly as he'd arrived.

Chapter 9

NORMALLY I QUITE LIKED working closing shifts because of how cruisy they were.

Not tonight though.

Tonight's cruisy could go fuck itself. And why? Because the overwhelming quiet of this cruisy shift was letting me dwell on things I'd rather not think about:

Gavin.

And Gavin.

And more fucking Gavin.

How was I ever going to get through my shift without sneaking into the restroom and having a sneaky wank? My face was flushed, and it was impossible to drag my thoughts away from dirty stepdad fantasies and my pulsing cock.

"You okay, Mike?" Chad looked at me quizzically, his head tilted.

"I'm fine." I looked back at my hipster coworker, startled. "Just feeling a little hot. Is the air conditioning working right?"

"As right as it ever is." He grinned. "Is it all good with you if I go take my break now?"

The fact we were the only two people in the bar should have given him the answer. "Yeah. I'll be fine."

He plucked out a joint he had stashed in his pocket and made his way out back towards the alleyway. While Chad's lack of professionalism bugged me at times, I couldn't help but wish he'd come back and tell me one of his outlandish travel stories to give my mind something to focus on other than Gavin.

In an effort to stop myself crushing on a man who was both morally and sexually unachievable, I thought about Jockey and how sexy and spontaneous he'd been at the park this morning. So what if I still had doubts about how the redneck stoner planned to use me. At least he would do so honestly, and I would never be left wondering what I meant to him. I was his faggot. His fuckhole. His possession. And considering Gavin intended on marrying Fiona, and therefore moving on with his life, it was important my needy ass had someone I could cling to when that happened.

I wonder if he's popped the question to Fiona yet?

That was the wrong thing to think about. Almost immediately my mind was drowning in images of Gavin walking about the kitchen in just a pair of boxers. I pictured those toned, brown legs of his, hairy chest, strong arms wrapped around me, and the lush curls in his armpits that I was desperate to sniff and lick.

I chided myself for revelling in such a taboo fantasy and cursed the boner inside my pants that refused to surrender. To distract myself from thoughts of Gavin, I reached into my jeans pocket and pulled out the note Jockey had given me in the park this morning. If I was going to be stuck behind a bar whilst nursing a hard-on, then I'd rather that hard-on be fuelled by images of someone I could actually have sex with.

Hey faggot

While technically you don't need to be using permission slips until our contract officially starts, I still think it would be handy for you to use one if you do fuck about. This way you can collect the man's details and give it back to me so I can store it in your fag file.

As explained in the contract you signed, I will be maintaining a complete record of every man who fucks you. Think of it like someone keeping hold of any invoices from a mechanic who works on their car. You are the car and every time a man puts his cock under your bonnet, I need to make sure it is recorded. Just like I have recorded the results from your STD test. This is important because if I choose to sell you on to a new owner then he needs to know just how much milage there is on you. Before you have a bitch fit about this, I want you to know I have no plans of selling you anytime soon. You still have plenty of tread left in your tires that I plan on wearing down.

Now remember. It is YOUR responsibility to make sure that any man who fucks you provides the correct information. You should know better than anyone how certain males like to exaggerate their TRUE cock size. So if in doubt make him measure his dick in front of you.

You might also like to know that my revenge plan on Damian has worked perfectly. I knew it would. A good soldier always completes his mission.

Love and kisses bitch

The tone of the note was infuriating, and had pissed me off when I had first read it, but I'd be lying if I said it didn't turn me on. There was a dark thrill in knowing it was written by a man I once thought of as a joke and beneath me. For some reason that only made the idea of submitting to Jockey even hotter. Like I was finally being taught a lesson I deserved.

But do I deserve this? Being compared to a motor vehicle?

I didn't know. But I was locked in now if I liked it or not. For the next twelve months my life would revolve around Jockey's cock, and untold hours spent on my knees between his wiry thighs. Anytime I considered putting an end to our arrangement, and I had numerous times, I quickly remembered his warning about how if I ended the contract without paying him compensation then he would make me regret it. I believed him too, especially after how he'd set Damian up the way he had.

I was about to read the note again when a voice blowed in from the entrance—"Good evening, Michael," I heard. "You look lonely there on your own." I quickly stuffed the note back in my pocket, and I turned around to see a very unwanted punter—Brian's father.

Dressed in black dress pants, white shirt, and an eye-catching blue and yellow tie, Rowan Quayle looked every bit the legal professional that he was. Toning down the corporate getup—in a good way—was a brown leather jacket that somehow managed to be both youthful and age-appropriate for the sixty-year-old. Mrs Quayle's influence for sure.

He wasted no time strolling right over to the bar. "Is it just you here on your own?"

"No," I lied. "My manager is out back." *Out back in the alley smoking a joint.*

Rowan looked in the direction of the kitchen. "Are they? I can't see anyone back there."

"That means he must be upstairs in the office."

The smug smile on Rowan's face suggested he could tell I was lying. As he took a seat right across from me, I braced myself for whatever sleezy pickup line he'd been dying to use on me. I had half a mind to undo my manbun and use my long blond locks to curtain my face so I wouldn't have to look at him. Thankfully he kept any lewd thoughts to himself. He then very politely ordered a gin and tonic before starting to tell me about how busy his day had been.

As I mixed Mr Quayle his drink, I prayed that Chad would get his ass back here pronto. But that was unlikely. He'd only left for his break ten minutes ago and he always took at least an hour.

I handed Mr Quayle his drink and quickly picked up a cloth and pretended like the other end of the bar was in desperate need of wiping down. I shuffled around, dumb-faced, doing my best to try and look busy.

To my relief, the man didn't say a word. Didn't even look at me. Just sat there quietly sipping his gin and tonic.

I couldn't look at him without picturing grey pubes and the soft droop of his baby boomer cock that I'd so hungrily sucked off in the public toilets. To be fair, I don't think he had grey pubes from what I could recall, and he certainly hadn't been soft and droopy at the time. Instead, he had thrusted his erection through that glory hole into my gaping mouth with the strength and stamina of someone my age.

It seemed hard to believe that just last week I had gone to Hickford Park determined to find him so I could hate-fuck his asshole. Foolishly, I had thought it would be the perfect way to get revenge against Brian. I wasn't thinking straight at the time, and hindsight made it quite clear that it had never been a good idea. What good would fucking an old man achieve? Nothing. That's what.

I soon found myself thinking about Brian, wondering why after so many years of friendship the four-eyed prick had ghosted me. And had now also blocked me. Even though I knew I shouldn't, a part of me still missed him. He'd been my more socially acceptable friend, the guy who I thought *got me*, just like I had always assumed I got him. But maybe that had never been the case.

The more I questioned why Brian had cut me off the closer I found myself drifting towards his father, as if subconsciously I thought the older man might have some answers.

"Can I ask you something, Mr Quayle?"

His blue eyes met mine, unwaveringly. "We've been over this, Mike. Please just call me Rowan. And yes you can ask me a question. You don't need my permission for that."

"The thing is...I haven't heard from Brian since he moved away to uni and I just wondered if you know what it is I've done to upset him?"

Rowan's voice came out casual and slow, like he was feigning boredom, "I wouldn't worry too much about that. My son is just being an ignoramus."

"It's got to be more than that. He's even blocked me on social media. So I must have done something to upset him."

"Trust me, Mike, you have not done anything wrong. It's Brian who is the problem. I haven't spoken with him either since he moved away. In fact, he's only called home twice and both times it was just to ask his mother for money. Quick and brief. Selfish. Very selfish."

"But I thought you and Mrs Quayle had planned to go up and see him?"

"We had. But he sent his mother an email asking us not to come up. Said he would be too busy to spend any time with us." Rowan chuckled humourlessly. "Which is quite rich considering he's not too busy to spend our money."

That didn't sound like Brian I know. He'd always adored his parents, and hadn't been one of those rich kids who bled his parents dry. Was he spoilt? For sure. But not selfishly so. Well...he never used to be.

"That doesn't sound too good," I said.

Mr Quayle dismissed my concern with a smile. "It's fine. I want Brian to enjoy himself. He's just doing what young people do when they move away from home for the first time. They get a bit too wrapped up in their own lives, not realising how hurtful they are being. I am sure he will come to his senses soon."

Maybe that was true. But it didn't take away the pain Brian had caused me.

We talked for another ten minutes, and it was like our encounter at Hickford Park had never happened. The talk was clean, although a little dry at times, but entirely appropriate. This was the Mr Quayle I had known and liked; an educated man who seemed to take a genuine interest in what I was doing with my life. He could be a bit preachy about the importance of hard work and education but I didn't mind. I just liked knowing that someone as successful as he was thought I was capable of doing great things if I put my mind to it.

When he was about to finish his drink, Mr Quayle said, "Here...take this."

I stared at the twenty dollar note in his hand. "What's that for?"

"Your tip. I know it's not the Kiwi way but I like to reward excellent service, and yours, Mike, is excellent."

I was about to put the money in the tip jar when I realised there was a small handwritten note beneath the cash.

I am housesitting for a friend in town at 228 Carrington Street. I would love it if you popped around after work tonight to keep me company. If you decide to stay the night I can drop you home in the morning. It is your choice but I have one thousand good reasons for you in my pocket why you should.

Finished reading the note, I glanced up to see Rowan about to stand up and leave. "Is this for real?"

Rowan nodded.

"And when you say a thousand good reasons you do mean—"

"A thousand dollars. Yes. I told you last time I was here that I believe you are top shelf quality and that I would pay accordingly."

"You'll pay me *that* much money just to have sex with you? Are you crazy?"

"There is nothing crazy about your beauty, Michael. If I have to pay to experience the pleasure your body has to offer then I will. My only regret is I cannot give you more...right now anyway."

"But that's a lot of money."

He smiled in assent, with tight, thin lips; a stunning white flash. "I know."

I stared back at him with a knot of shame burning in my gut. I don't know why I was the one who was embarrassed. I hadn't written the note. But I swear you could fry an egg on my face it was that hot.

"I don't know what to say," I told him.

"I would like it if you say yes."

Self-respect aside, I was rather flattered at the idea of being paid so much money for sex. I then found myself undressing Mr Quayle with my eyes. If I ignored the fact he was sixty, I guess it wasn't *all* bad. He wasn't fat, was unlikely to be rocking a Chewbacca body, and he wasn't what I would call ugly. If anything he was just Brian in forty years, and I had always wanted to fuck Brian.

My voice dropped to a whisper and I leaned close. "What would I have to do?"

"I would like to give you a nice rub down. A full body massage. We would suck one another off, and I would of course expect to fuck you for that kind of money."

"Would you use a condom?"

"Of course. Protection is always best."

That was good. I would score a thousand bucks *and* be able to supply Jockey with the used rubber he was so desperate for me to give him. I glanced at the note again, my heart beating fast. Was I actually going to agree to this? Was I going to let myself be tainted with another unenviable label? I didn't want to be like Damian. I was better than that. But—

A thousand dollars!!!

"Well, you have the address," Mr Quayle said placidly, as if he was unconcerned what my answer would be. "I hope to see you later."

I nodded, unable to speak, and watched him walk out the door with a triumphant grin on his face.

Chapter 10

WHAT THE HELL AM I doing?

It wasn't the first time I had asked myself that question since leaving work. More than once I considered turning back, but I reminded myself about Jockey's note and his demand to be given a used condom. Although one part of my mind laughed at my foolishness, my instincts had lured me here, and I could only assume I was going to go through with it.

Seriously. What the hell am I doing?

Silencing my inner voice, I climbed the front steps and knocked on the door. When thirty seconds passed with no answer, I told myself it was a sign that I should leave. I was about to do just that when I heard footsteps approaching from inside and the door swung open.

Stood on the doorstep like a stunned meerkat, heart pounding in my ears, my ability to speak was momentarily gone. The reality of what I had come here to do had finally hit me. My body tingled with a flush.

"Mike?" Trent looked more than a little surprised to see me. He was still wearing his work clothes: brown boots, blue jeans and a white-shirt that needed a date with the washing machine. He took a squizz behind me to see if I was alone. "Is Gavin with you?"

"Uh, no. It's just me," I replied, trying to keep the blood down below my neck. "I was in the neighbourhood so I thought I'd stop by."

He tipped me a wandering glance from face to feet, but said nothing. He had every right to be suspicious. I never came here unless I was with Gavin. Never.

"I brought beer," I said, hefting the six-pack.

"So you did." He eyed the label of the beer, then me again. It felt like a small eternity passed before I finally heard him say the words, "Come in."

I'm not sure of the exact moment I decided to come to Trent's house. It just sort of happened. One minute I was on my way to meet Mr Quayle and the next I started walking in the other direction. At some point I must have decided I'd rather risk getting a punch to the face than get paid a thousand dollars to let Brian's father fuck me. I still wasn't sure why Trent was my cock's target. The only reason I could come up with was his link to Gavin, and maybe if I shagged Trent then it would help banish those dirty, dirty thoughts about my stepfather. As idiotic as this last-minute plan was, it felt better than adding whore to my sexual resume. I needed to draw the line somewhere, and I decided that line was sucking dick for cash.

Trent led me downstairs to the mancave and immediately made his way over to the pool cues on the wall. "I'm guessing you've come back for a rematch. Gavin's always said you're a competitive little bugger."

"Sounds about right," I said.

It felt like the Kentucky Darby inside my chest. If I was this nervous just being inside the house then I wondered how on earth I'd have the balls to ask the man for a fuck.

Despite having a puppy-like playfulness about him, Trent still managed to radiate parochial small-town vibes. The sort of bloke made insecure by a soy latte and words with syllables. That's not to say he was part of the bigot brigade by any means, but he had never struck me as openminded or as liberal as Gavin. Instead, I always got the impression that Trent just followed Gavin's lead. If I were to use some of Jockey's terminology then I suppose I'd describe Trent as the beta to Gavin's alpha.

For the next hour we played pool while I tried to build up the courage to go through with my plan, which admittedly was pretty non-existent. Other than envisioning the pair of us ending up in bed, I hadn't given it much thought how we would get there.

Whenever Trent lined up to take a shot, my eyes wandered over his physique. The t-shirt tucked into his belted blue jeans showcased his beer belly (probably hairy, too, if his arms were any indication). The rest of his body looked less doughy thankfully. Decent legs. Strong arms. Feet, looking bigger than their actual size because of those sooty work boots. The magnet of his package kept drawing my glances: nice, full relief of dick and balls packed in denim.

More than once I worried that he had caught me scoping him out, but he never said anything. Just mouthed down more guzzles of beer, telling me endless stories about some of the houses he had worked on over the past year. I kept waiting for the right moment to say something that might get the ball rolling in a sexual direction, but as the minutes ticked by, slowly and mockingly, I began to realise there was no right moment.

Trent started droning on about the new subdivision being developed on the edge of town. The first I'd heard about the subdivision—pretentiously named by the developers as Pacific

Heights despite the land being flat as a pancake—was a year ago when Brian had excitedly informed me that his parents had bought two of the sections there with the intent of building themselves rental properties. There was nothing quite so quintessentially Kiwi these days as an overpriced property market fuelled by rich boomers like Brian's parents adding to their ever-growing property portfolios. When Brian had told me of his parents' purchase, I had nodded and smiled through resentment. Right now though, I was smiling and nodding through how fucking disinterested I was in the cost of ordering building supplies from Australia.

While Trent rambled at length about building codes, I allowed myself to imagine what was going on behind that buttoned zipper of his. After sinking one the balls, he stepped back to survey the table and unashamedly adjusted his package. I tore my eyes off his crotch and choked down a dry swallow.

"Their cookie-cutter cheap, and made of unnatural building materials," he said, lining up for his next shot.

"Are we talking about the houses or the rich housewives moving into them?" My eyes were on his crotch when I said this.

"Both," he chuckled. "Some of them are right plastic bitches moving in up there."

While Trent resumed the dull topic of building codes, it dawned on me that my decision to come here tonight was culminating into a huge flashing *FML* sign. There was no way I was going to get a fuck out of this man if this was all he could talk about. The only consolation was the sound of his voice which I'd decided was sexier than I had ever realised. It had a sort of masculine, playful growl, and lessened the pain of such a boring topic. Naturally, it got me wondering how that voice must sound in the bedroom, when breaking commandments and grunting alternate takes on Heaven.

Suck my fuckin' cock! Yeah, like that. Now lick the sweat off my nuts! Can't wait to bend you over. Fuck you in the ass, fucker!

"It's not that big," Trent said, cutting through my sexy daydream.

"Huh?"

"My dick," he said, his voice distorting into a feral growl. "You've been staring at it long enough, so you gotta know it's pretty average."

A jolt of ice cut through my heated body. Had I just heard him correctly?

Our eyes met and I was on the verge of dropping the pool stick and running up the stairs and out the front door.

Trent laughed, a snarl of a smile appearing on his face. "Oh, Mike. You should see your face right now, mate."

"What?"

"I'm just yanking your chain. I know you're looking at the belt. It's pretty cool aye?" He sucked in his belly to give me a better look at the buckle. "Donna bought it for me last Christmas. Said she was sick and tired of me walking around with saggy pants."

While I was relieved not to have been caught scoping out his goods, I couldn't help but feel that it was now or never. This man was too innocent to be led astray unless I just came out with it.

"Actually," I started nervously. "You were right the first time. I've been looking at your dick."

"That's a good one." He rolled is eyes. "You can't prank a prankster, buddy."

"It's not a prank. The reason I'm here tonight is to see if you fancied watching Die-Hard with me."

His brow wrinkled in confusion. "I suppose we can do that. But it doesn't have to be Die-Hard. We can find something else on Netflix if you want."

"What I mean is *you* watch Die-Hard while *I* make you feel good."

"What are you on about?"

I responded in caveman English: "I. Want. To. Suck. Your. Dick."

Trent's hairy throat knotted under the influence of a heavy swallow. His voice lower, calmer, he answered, "Is that why you came here tonight? So you could..."

I finished the sentence for him. "Suck your cock."

Any lingering confusion vanished and I saw the face of a man caught off guard. He didn't look happy about it. I suppose he had every right to be angry. Here I was, the teenaged son of his best friend, dropping by unannounced and propositioning him in his own home.

My mind rattled its cage, screaming to the rest of my body that I had to abort the mission before it was too late. I didn't heed any of the warnings though. I let whatever dark nasty force working its magic on me tug me closer to my stepfather's best friend. My eyes darted from his icy gaze to the crotch of his sweaty and smudged jeans.

I stepped closer. For a second I thought he was going to push me away, maybe even throw a punch. Instead he took my hand in his and stuffed my fingers behind his jeans and across the cotton of his underwear. I let it happen, feeling the mound of his flesh in my palm beneath the fabric.

He wasn't hard, and I wondered for a moment if he was tricking me. But I was cupping his cock and balls. My hand was in his pants. Instinctively I gave him a small squeeze, rubbing at the flaccid lump in my hand.

Working around my groping hand, Trent unbuttoned the fly of his jeans with ease, just like he would have if he were about to take a piss at a urinal. He leaned in close. I could feel the heat of his breath on my neck.

"Get on your knees," he said flatly, "and have a taste."

A strong, hairy forearm came to rest on my shoulder. A single hand cradled the back of my head. Even as I sank to the floor, I was in disbelief. This was actually happening. This was Trent. Gavin's best mate. I was touching him. And I was about to do something I'd never until today imagined doing, to Trent. A father and married man!

Donna's face flashed in my mind but fluttered away. I was staring right at the swell in Trent's threadbare underwear. My fingers trembled when I pulled the flaps of his jeans aside. I tugged them lower to get a good look. A rich aroma filled my every breath. It wasn't unpleasant. Wadded into the fabric of his briefs I saw the outline of his cock, the round rim of the head, and the mound of balls tucked beneath.

I pulled Trent's jeans down to the tops of his boots, revealing his tighty-whities in all their well-worn glory. I inhaled the musty smell of a real man's crotch and almost ejaculated without even touching my dick.

The intoxicating scent of unwashed balls; hard, sweaty cock; and lush pubes spoke to me. High on Trent's smell, I went on automatic. One hand fondled the prominent bulge inside his briefs. The other stroked a length of hairy leg from calf to thigh. Trent moaned. A calloused hand on the back of my skull held me in place. The more I mouthed him through the threadbare fabric the more I felt his sex grow.

"Oh man," Trent exhaled. "You better start sucking before I come to my senses and change my mind."

Urged by that warning, I dragged the man's underwear down to his boots. Distant thoughts about the morality of what I was doing protested, but to no avail. It happened so fast. My face was filled with transgressive flesh. Soft pubes brushed against my skin. Trent's growing hardness was mashed against my cheek. As if programmed, I opened my mouth, and lapped at whatever flesh was there.

One hand bracing on his leg for support, I closed my eyes and sucked his cock down to the curls, inhaling the raw, wonderful odour of his balls between gulps. His erection flexed on my tongue, and for an instant I swore I could feel the pulse of circulation inside it, the blood and excitement surging through, spurred on by rapid heartbeats and lust for me. His cock was full of life, and having it in my mouth made me feel alive as well.

Trent held my head against his crotch, but not forcefully so. His hand merely encouraged that I stay. His fingers rubbed and groped through my hair, and it made me feel welcome to do whatever I pleased with my mouth. So I did.

The head of his dick suddenly popped from my lips. I looked up from my place on the floor. Trent stared down at me; his mouth open. I could still see the corner of his lips pulled up into a grin. I felt awkward in that moment. I'd slipped into a trance and indulged myself. Trent looking back at me made this real. His impossibly blue eyes spoke louder than any words.

Then, as if to make sure I knew how committed he was to letting me suck his cock, he stepped back and removed all his clothes. Stood before me fully naked, I finally got a chance to take in the male specimen that was Trent Pembroke. His chest was covered in a masculine forest of dark curls, as were his legs. I was certainly partial to a bit of body hair on a man but Trent was undoubtedly the hairiest dude I had ever seen naked in real life.

He stepped back towards me and both of my hands clutched the round cheeks of his ass. I squeezed them and pulled him in, gagging myself with his hard dick.

"Oh fuck, Mike!" Trent groaned at me through his teeth.

Trent's hips drove into my head and back again. He worked with a slow methodical rhythm. I felt each swing of his hairy balls when they hit my chin. It wasn't too much to handle. I met each slow thrust greedily.

Reluctantly, I released his cock, but only to lick at his balls. The taste of his sweat was much stronger here. More dank. More dark. More male. It suddenly occurred to me that this hairy, wrinkled sac I was licking contained a fountain of life. I don't know why but it felt a privilege to suck on such fertile flesh. Trent Pembroke's balls really were babymakers. Perhaps it was a reminder to me how he usually put his cock in very different places.

He leaked rivers, nectar of the gods. I sucked his dick, bathed his nuts, massaged a hairy calf with the hand that should have been trying to free my own dick from solitary confinement. But as magical as all this was, I couldn't let him lose his lollies before putting a condom on him.

I pulled away. "Before you cum there's something I need you to do."

"What's that?" he puffed.

"I need you to fuck me."

I expected push back, some straight guy excuse that it was a step too far.

"I think that can be arranged," he said, the snarl of that sexy smile playing crookedly at one corner of his mouth. "But only if you promise to stay the night so I can fuck you again in the morning."

I went to put his cock back in my mouth but he stepped away. "Not so fast, tiger." He chuckled. "If we're both agreed this is an all night scenario then let's take our time and enjoy ourselves."

"Won't you enjoy it more with your cock in my mouth?"

Trent laughed. "I imagine I would. But what's the rush? We've got all night. Perhaps we could sit down and watch a movie together first?" He walked over to a shelf on the wall and fetched from it a bottle of whiskey and two glasses. "I was saving this for Gavin and Fiona but I think it's better if you and me drink it. Whattaya say?"

"I say..." I jumped to my feet. "Yippee-ki-yay, motherfucker!"

Chapter 11

I WOKE UP TO BARITONE snores and my face pressed against hairy skin. Trent's furry chest to be precise. Sunlight filtered through the gaps of the curtains, bright enough to indicate the day outside was well underway. Trent's beefy arm was hooked around my waist; keeping me close while he dreamed.

With painstaking caution, I lifted my head to squint at the room. We weren't in the basement anymore but in one of the upstairs bedrooms. When I saw a family photo on the wall, I realised I was naked in what had once been Trent and Donna's marital bed. And judging by the feel of the scorching hot morning wood pressing against my thigh, I wasn't the only one who was naked.

Just how far did things go last night?

That's when I noticed a big patch of dried cum on my belly, a satisfied tingle in the ass accompanied by a slight pain—telltale signs that a cock had been in there. Investigating further, I could feel a cum stain on the sheet between my legs where jism had drained from my hole. I was somewhat saddened by the knowledge I had obviously had a real good fucking and that it was missing from my memory bank, but I was also mad at myself for once again letting a man nut inside me.

With the gentleness of a whisper, I lifted Trent's arm in slow motion, watching his face for any signs of change. Millimetre by millimetre, I rolled away from his hairy flesh toward the edge of the bed. It was a weekday and I was pretty fucking sure that Trent had slept in and was seriously late for work.

Perched on the side of the bed like a disoriented canary, I cradled my dizzy head in my hands, trying to remember what had unfolded last night. I could remember sucking his dick—the size and taste of it—and I remembered drinking whiskey on the couch while watching Die-Hard. But after that...

It was all a blank.

Trent was still breathing deeply, so I figured I'd better pee, cleanup a bit, dress, and be gone before he woke up. Even if he remembered what we had done last night, I wasn't sure I wanted to hang around to witness his straight male regret and its coinciding meltdown.

After a satisfactory piss, and a quick splash of water to the face, I came out of the en suite to find Trent leaning up on his elbows in bed. His cowlick and a clump of hair hanging down over his brow gave him an air of innocence belied by the hard meat very evident beneath the sheet. His nipples were hard and pointed, sticking through though the thick mat of hair on his chest.

"Morning, stud," he said, following it up with a flirty smile. "We got pretty shitfaced last night, didn't we?"

Realising he wasn't headed for some sort of *I'm-not-a-fucking-queer* meltdown, I allowed myself to relax. "You can say that again. I can barely remember a thing."

"All you have to know is we had a lot of fun." He moistened his lips with a flash of his wet pink tongue. "And I do mean *a lot* of fun."

"I'm glad one of us remembers."

"Take it from me, Mike, you are one feisty firecracker of a fuck."

"I am?"

"Yeah, mate. Last night would be some of the friskiest action I've had in years. Donna was never one for dirty talk so it was nice to be reminded that I've got a big dick."

The room went quiet and I was unsure how to proceed with this morning after limbo I found myself in. My sudden anxiety wasn't helped by the fact he kept looking at my crotch; my naked cock and balls.

Desperate to kill the quiet, I asked him, "Aren't you missing work?"

"I'm my own boss, remember? So we've got the rest of the day for more fun if you're keen to hang around."

A wordless nod was all I could manage.

"Seriously, Mike, I can't thank you enough for last night. Not just because it was great sex but because you restored my confidence."

"I did?"

"Yeah. I know it might sound silly but with me and Donna separating I've been nervous as fuck about dipping my foot back into the pool again. The last time I was single I was in my early twenties with a thirty-one-inch waist and six-pack abs. Things have changed a bit since then, and not just my body, but you made me feel like a stud again." He then added with a smirk, "Even if it was the booze talking."

"Someone can be drunk and still tell the truth."

"That's true. You certainly shared enough of your secrets last night."

"What sort of secrets?"

"Well, you admitted to me that you have a big old crush on Gav. Said you used to shoot his cum up your ass you with a water pistol."

Oh my fuck!

Heat baked off my cheeks. Just how much had I had to drink last night?"

Trent smiled, a slow dirty smile. "You also said something about how you've signed a sex contract with a friend of yours. Apparently you're now his property for the next twelve months."

"Was that whiskey or truth serum you gave me?"

"Don't worry," he chuckled. "I ain't gonna tell no one."

"Thanks."

"To be honest I was thinking you were telling porkies about that contract business but I'm guessing it's legit?"

"Yeah."

"I'm glad," he replied as he rolled over to grab something from the bedside table. "It means filling this out last night wasn't a waste of time."

"Huh?"

He handed me what he'd picked up. A blue piece of paper. My stomach knotted. It was one of Jockey's consent forms I'd had in my pocket.

"It has my physical stats you asked for," Trent said. "You said you might need them so this master of yours can put them in your *fag file*. Your words not mine."

I glanced over the answers Trent had given. I couldn't decide what impressed me more; the fact he'd filled in the form or that he appeared to have given honest answers. Nothing seemed embellished.

Name: MYOB
Age: 36
Height: *5 ft 6*
Hair colour: *Brown*
Eyes: *Hazel*
Physique: *I could benefit from losing 20 pounds but I'm still quite muscular.*
Cock size. *6.5 inches*
Thickness: *Above average.*
Cut or uncut: *Uncut*
Shoe size: *8*
Balls: *Big baby makers lol*
Body hair: *Hairier than average.*

It was the section at the bottom of the consent form that made me cringe the most. The one titled: **Feedback on the faggot.**

Mike was a lot of fun and more than happy to please me. Not only is he a great kisser but he's also really good at sucking dick and couldn't stop telling me how much he loved my cock. He also deserves brownie points for giving my balls a good lick.

During our first fuck the condom broke (I was a bit too eager so my bad) and I came in his ass. Mike's the only person I've fucked in quite a while so I wouldn't get too excited about that. And as potent as my boys are I doubt I got him up the duff haha

I fucked his ass another two times and gave him a load of my 'daddy juice' (as Mike liked to call it) down his throat. The first fuck (the one when the rubber broke) was doggy style but the next two were him on his back with his ankles over my shoulders. I've always been really into kissing during sex so it shouldn't be a surprise to learn that I liked him more on his back. The other benefit to that position was being able to see his eyes roll back each time I hit him deep. Mmm.

"Great," I huffed. "So apparently when I get drunk I don't just share my secrets, but I also refer to cum as *daddy juice*."

"Considering how fertile my balls seem to be you ain't wrong to call it that."

"I'm not sure that makes it any better."

"I wouldn't stress about that. It's all part of your charm."

"If by charm you mean embarrassing, then yeah... I'm full of it."

"When a lad's got a body as good as yours they shouldn't feel embarrassed about anything."

"Get off the grass. My body's not that good."

"It was good enough to get me to fuck boy ass for the first time in my life, so that should tell you something."

I wanted to take the compliment but instead I was overcome with suspicion. "Are you sure last night was your first time?"

"I've dabbled in the past but never gone that far. Nowhere near it."

"When you say dabbled are you talking about kissing Gavin at parties?"

"Nar. I did stuff with another mate of ours. Handjobs mostly. It was years ago though. Back at high school." He smiled faintly, politely. "What made you think I'd fucked a man before?"

"You just seem very relaxed about it all. I mean, shouldn't you be running to the basin to wash your mouth out and screaming at me to get out of the house?"

He laughed. "Okay, for starters I'm not a fuckwit. And second, I've always felt relaxed around you. Ever since you were a little dude. You're non-threatening. And I don't mean in a pussy way. You just have a kind vibe about you. It's nice...you're nice."

The compliment felt good and helped dissolve some of the guilt and shame I felt bubbling inside. While it was clear Trent and Donna's marriage was on the rocks it didn't change the fact I'd assisted in the committing of a marital sin.

"Thanks, Trent." I smiled. "You're nice too."

"I probably should be shitting myself considering I just spent all night scuttling my best mate's boy. Gavin would have a fucking hernia if he found out."

"You don't have to worry about that because I don't plan on him finding out."

"I'm glad we agree on that."

We fell silent again, and I began to wonder how we would act the next time we were in the same room as Gavin. How good would we be at pretending last night never happened? Would it be awkward?

Trent turned onto his back, one hairy leg outside the covers. He stretched and yawned, folded his arms behind his head. The black whorls in his pits almost bridged the mat on his chest.

"So you've just read how I found last night," he said, "but what about you? Did you enjoy yourself? Did I give it to you the way you like it?"

"You tell me. Last night is a complete blur."

"Is that an invitation to refresh your memory?" Trent waggled his eyebrows.

It hadn't been, but I hesitated before saying so. I inched closer to the bed and quite slowly, savouring the revelation, pulled the sheet down as Trent's gleaming, toothy grin grew larger. The wide band of fur on his belly narrowed somewhat below the navel where it fed down to a forest of bush, matted and stained by the previous evening's revel. Beneath the morning wood of thick cock his balls lay quiet against his body, not stirring in their hairy sac, but definitely ready for any kind of action I could invent.

I started to run my fingertips, feather light, over his body, beginning in his armpit, and working over his chest and arms, teasing his nipples with a soft touch that soon had his skin jumping where I caressed it. He began to squirm under my hands, and make fucking motions with his hips. His breathing became irregular but he remained in place, content to let me explore his body.

And that was the keyword here: *explore*.

In recent years I had dismissed this man as a friendly knuckle-dragger with a chunky and unfit body. But now, viewing Trent as an offering of naked flesh, I was again realising I'd been too harsh in my judgement. He wasn't model fit by any means, nor was he the sharpest tool in the shed, but he radiated a blue-collar sex appeal that I was learning more and more was right up my alley.

My sweaty palms worked their way farther down, over his hairy beer belly and around his dick, which was fully erect, and throbbed in the air with each heartbeat. The thick shaft was not straight, but curved upward, and the blood that pumped through it darkened the head to a swollen bluish purple. I worked lightly over his balls, made them jump and roll under my fingers, and then invaded his crotch, tickling his asshole and stroking the tight, wrinkled muscle until he pressed down and it puckered under my fingertip. He laughed, showing me his teeth.

While my fingers toyed with his ass hair—withholding the urge to dig inside his sweat-moistened hole—my eyes wandered down his pale legs to his even paler feet. They weren't things of beauty; wide, flat, adorned with square toes, and a blister on one heel; they were simply tools he used to stand on. But I still took a snapshot in my mind, determined to memorise as much of his body as I could.

When I returned my gaze to Trent's cock, I saw that his slit was flowing, dripping down over his stomach, and I rubbed my fingers in the clear, slippery fluid, and used it to lubricate them as I began to trace patterns on his thigh.

By this time, he was fucking the air with his hips, lunging and straining as if he were buried in my throat or my asshole. Even his toes were flexing, and the muscles stood out on his hairy legs.

Putting an end to my exploration, Trent sat up and sucked my nipple into his mouth, sparking a chain reaction of hot explosions that settled in my gut and hardened my dick. I felt him smile against me before slowly pulling away with one last flick of his tongue against my nipple.

"Come back to bed," he whispered. "You may not remember this but you promised me a morning fuck."

Funnily enough, that was one of the few things I did remember. And in this moment, I could think of nothing better than honouring that promise.

But I needed to use the toilet first.

"Let me use the loo real quick," I said. "I'm a bit full after last night."

"Can't you take a shit afterwards?"

"It's not that." I felt my cheeks redden. "I just need to get rid of what you put up there."

He stared at me and asked, almost wonderingly, "Is that all?"

"What do you mean *is that all*?" I pointed to the stain I'd left on the bed. "I leaked all over the sheets, and it still feels like I've got a pint of milk up there."

The smile returned to his handsome, stubbled face. He paused, for a brief moment, as if to gauge my sincerity, then yanked me onto the bed.

"What are you doing?" I half-laughed as he spun me about like a ragdoll, positioning me so that I was practically sat over his chest and facing the foot of the bed.

"I'm gonna clean up the mess I made."

I wondered what the hell he was on about until he clutched my hips and dragged my ass to his face. Fingers pried my cheeks open, and his breath washed hot across my moist hole.

"Oh, fuck," I grunted. He wasn't planning to—

My eyes rolled back in my head, and a muffled moan escaped me as Trent's tongue penetrated my asshole. The heat within me intensified as he explored my hole with a ravenous hunger while continuing to pull me onto his face.

While he sucked and slurped on my slippy hole, I leaned forward and took his swollen erection into my mouth. My shoulder-length hair fell like a blond veil in front of my face, stroking his thighs and pubes. I tasted lingering traces of my own asshole; a sweet earthiness I would have found revolting if it weren't my own.

Trent's hips lifted restlessly, chasing the hot wet suction of my mouth. I stroked him a few times, pumping as he writhed and moaned beneath me. I lowered my head and swallowed him right down to those coarse, wiry curls.

"Squeeze it out," he mouthed into my hole. "Feed me more of my daddy juice."

Those words, those dirty, dirty words, triggered something inside me, and I knew without a doubt I would honour and service this man's cock to the best of my ability.

Loosening my sphincter muscles, I gave him what he had asked for, and squeezed out the remains of his load. I feared the rasping sound of a fart, which thankfully never came. But I don't think it would have bothered Trent if it had; that's how committed he was to getting every drip of that ass-flavoured *daddy juice* onto his tongue.

Suddenly, Trent picked me up and spun me around with such ease I might as well have been a toy. He clutched my head with both hands and rolled us over so I was now on my back with him on top of me. His lips smashed against mine, and I tasted the deepest, darkest part of me on his lips.

"I've gotta fuck you again," he whispered. "I *need* to fuck you, Mike."

His voice, so low and urgent and passionate, spoke to the most male parts of my body and soul. I placed a hand on either side of his face and sucked his tongue back into my mouth, giving him my consent. Trent then got up and rifled through the bedside drawers, retrieving a condom and a small, finger-smudged bottle of lube. I wondered if these were from a time when he and Donna had still been intimate with each other, and if so were they out of date?

I silenced those thoughts and watched as he rolled the yellowy rubber down his throbbing prick before coating it with a generous amount of lubricant. He then lay down on the bed, on his back, and beckoned me to squat over him.

I did so, swaying slightly as I got into position. Fanning my slim thighs wide, I held my balls in one hand and leaned back on the other, affording Trent the perfect view as he lined his cock up with my asshole.

I lowered down enough to create some pressure against my anus. The fat knob was pressing against my hole, but didn't seem to be able to break through. Trent placed his hands on my thighs, and encouraged me to relax and let him in. I took a deep breath and sat down a little more firmly, and my sphincter began to open a bit.

When he gave a gentle nudge, the head popped through the ring of my ass muscles, and slipped right inside my hole.

"Shit!" I gasped, surprised by the sudden entry.

"You alright?" he asked, hands resting on my hips.

"Yeah. I'm fine."

After a few quick breaths, I nodded and let him know I was good to continue.

The man knew how to fuck, that's for sure. There was no sudden lunge, no feeling of I gotta show what a man I am. It was slow, with easy pushes against the locked ring, little tickling around the outer edge of my asshole, small squirming, and yet I sensed the strength of his beefy-muscled thighs and strong ass as they forced his cock slowly north inside my rectum.

Last night's action must have opened me up because the ring eventually gave way as if someone had turned a key, and he slid in, groaning with pleasure. I didn't feel too bad myself. His cock, once in, seemed larger and more satisfying somehow. My asshole was distended pleasurably, and in that position as he slowly moved straight in he hit my joy spot head on. I moved my head back, neck muscles straining, and moaned involuntarily.

"Did I hurt you?" he asked softly.

"Anything...but," I gasped. "You... hit it... just right."

He started to screw me. There was nothing fancy about it. No side movements, no poking around, just a wonderful straight in-and-out fuck. Unlike Jockey and Damian, Trent was fucking me in a way that gave us both pleasure. Maybe it was his age, gifting him some sexual maturity, or maybe it was because he didn't view his receptive partners as inferior. Perhaps both things were true.

I showed how grateful I was to have his respect by leaning forward and pressing our lips together, and sucking his tongue inside my mouth. He fed me a satisfied groan, stroking my rump tenderly. We stayed like that for a long moment—our lips locked and his cock fully embedded in my asshole.

When our kiss came to its natural end, I hoisted myself a few inches up off his dick, and the sensation of movement sent a wave of pleasure radiating through me, from my head to my toes. I shivered and moaned as I eased back down onto his hot, throbbing shaft. "Mmmm...."

Trent noticed the orgasmic tone in my voice. "Sounds like somebody's feeling pretty good, huh? You like having my dick up there?"

"Uh-huh, yeah." I said with a whimper.

I took his hands between my own and started sucking on his salty fingers as I pumped and rotated my ass on his cock. He could have broken loose, but he didn't; he waited; he let me do what I wanted to do, and I felt his hips squirm impatiently between my spread thighs. Then I let go of his hands and bent my head to kiss him again as I began fucking myself furiously on his cock.

I came like that, shuddering through long, copious spasms, bent over him, kissing him, his tongue in my throat, my long hair in his face. My dick left a scorching wetness all over his belly, the liquid heat sending him towards a climax of his own.

Trent muttered something like "oh baby" through our slowing kiss. His hips began thrashing as he lifted me off the bed with the strength and fury of his orgasm and within seconds he flooded the condom with a release that matched my own.

Finally we were spent. I was panting, sweating and trembling from the workout this man's cock had just given me. I was still too weak and shaky to try and move, and it didn't feel like my insides were ready to release Trent's cock just yet. I lay my cheek on his chest and listened to his heartbeat, matched by the throbbing I felt in my ass. Time stopped, and I felt like I was floating.

Beneath me, Trent lay perfectly still, with his hands resting on my butt cheeks. "That was amazing," he said and kissed me on the cheek.

I reflected on how this encounter—this fuck, and the three last night—would change things between us forever. It seemed remarkable to consider that, until twelve hours ago, Trent Pembroke had been like a surrogate uncle to me. Certainly not someone I had ever envisioned winding up naked and sweaty with. But here we were, now lumbered with a secret. And I sensed a treacherous road ahead.

Chapter 12

IT HAD RAINED OVERNIGHT, clearing the air and washing the streets. And as Trent drove me home, saving me from over an hour-long walk, I couldn't help but feel that the world looked different to me, a combination of the shining sidewalks, Trent's strong, fragrant aftershave and the secret we now shared.

As we neared my suburb I could feel Trent's growing anxiety. I'm not sure how much of it was fuelled by regret, but the lack of conversation in the vehicle suggested he needed some time to process what had happened. I didn't begrudge him for it. What we had done was a huge deal, and I imagined he probably had a lot of soul searching to do.

Rather than be dropped me off at home, I suggested he drop me off around the corner. I could tell he was relieved to hear that, probably worried about Gavin asking us unwanted questions.

Just before I stepped out of the car, Trent grabbed my arm and gave it an affectionate squeeze. "Hey, thanks again for last night, Mike. It was a lot of fun."

"It sure was."

"But you know we can't do it again, right?" His eyes looked almost pleading. "It was just a one-off. You know that, aye?"

I hesitated. "Uh, yeah. I know that."

"It's nothing against you but this really isn't my thing."

It felt like your thing an hour ago when your cock was in my—

"And you promise not to tell anyone?" he said. "I can't have Donna finding out. Not when we're on the verge of sorting out custody of the kids."

His concern for his children softened the blow, but not all of it. "I won't say a word."

"Cheers, mate." He smiled softly and licked his lips. "I can still taste your ass on my tongue. I gotta say it tastes pretty sexy."

That last part seemed such an odd thing to say considering it came on the heels of a rejection. Talk about mixed messages.

He let go of my arm and faced the road, letting me know our goodbye talk was over. I took one last glance at the crotch of his pants then slipped out of the vehicle.

Instead of walking home, I made my way towards Jockey's house instead, telling myself that it was important I hand him the filled-in permission slip right away. The redneck stoner usually finished work early on Thursdays and I hoped he'd be pleased to see me.

As I got closer to my master's abode, I realised that I wasn't just going there to hand over the permission slip, I was going because my needy ass didn't want to be alone. Not after feeling like I'd just been dumped while on a first date.

Trent's rejection shouldn't have bugged me so much. After all, I had only gone to his house with the intention of a one-night-stand. Yet his immediate pulling the plug on any potential encore performance left me wondering if I'd done something wrong. Had I accidentally come off too clingy? Had I been a crap lay? The used condom from this morning's romp that I'd smuggled away in my pocket suggested otherwise. But whatever the reason for the man's abrupt cooldown, I can't deny that my ego felt bruised.

Although I had sensed the road ahead would be treacherous after what Trent and I had done, it hadn't occurred to me that I would be walking it alone.

JOCKEY OPENED THE DOOR to his sleepout and revealed a cloud of pot smoke behind him. He stood there barefoot in just a pair of camo pants. A stoner glaze floated like pond scum over his eyeballs. Stepping into the skunky haze, my stomach did a little flip when I saw that he wasn't alone.

Sat on the couch was his brother Darren, long legs in ripped black jeans, each ending in a ratty sneaker. He too was rocking the shirtless look; his torso much paler than Jockey's sun-kissed skin. Like his baby brother, Darren Savage was a thin six-footer made up of sinewy muscles and a sharp face. Whereas Jockey's sharp features could look appealing, almost handsome if viewed on the right angle, Darren just looked like the sour-faced wannabe thug that he was.

"Mikey Mikester," Darren said in a slurred voice that told me he wasn't just stoned but drunk as well.

"Hi, Darren."

He stumbled up from the couch, nearly tripping over a row of empty beer cans, and came over to give me a bro-hug. "It's good to see you, brah."

I always thought you could tell a lot about a man by what word he used to greet you with. There was the good old-fashioned *mate*, the more youthful *bro*, the American-influenced *dude*, and then there was *brah*... the only one that bugged me on account of how fucking try-hard it sounded when spoken with a thick Kiwi accent—which Darren had.

Jockey stepped around us and took the spot on the couch vacated by his brother. After giving me two hard pats on the back, Darren released me from the unwanted hug and joined Jockey on the couch.

I dilly-dallied for a moment, unsure of where to sit. But commonsense told me Jockey wouldn't want me playing my role of owned faggot in front of his brother.

Turns out I was wrong.

"What are you doing, bitch," Jockey snapped when I went to sit down on the armchair. "Down here by my feet."

Face glowing with shame, I did as I was told.

"Don't be embarrassed, brah," Darren said. "Jockey's told me all about your guys arrangement. I'm doing the tattoo for you."

I had forgotten about that. Of course Darren knew. But that didn't lessen my embarrassment.

Darren then said, "I didn't believe it at first when Jockey told me you'd signed a contract to be his faggot. But he let me have a read of it earlier and I saw your signature and I just thought...wow... Michael freeman must really love the taste of dick."

"Something like that," I mumbled.

"Hey, ain't no shame in it," Darren said nonchalantly. "The world needs faggots just as much as it needs the alpha men who fuck them. It's the way the world works. You can't have one without the other."

Darren's odd rambling told me two things. One; he really was off his tits. And two; he clearly believed in this alpha fag bullshit every bit as his brother did. Shit, for all I knew he'd been the one to get Jockey into it.

"So have you decided where you're getting the tattoo?" Darren asked me.

"Not yet."

"Mike hasn't decided if he's even getting the tattoo," Jockey said, a snideness to his voice. "He may yet choose the other option."

Darren frowned. "The other option?"

"To let me video him getting bummed in Hickford Park."

Darren laughed. "Fuck that! Go with the tattoo, man. Definitely the tattoo."

Darren would be happy to know I was leaning more towards the tattoo option. The alternative was even more horrifying. I knew without a doubt that Jockey would upload any video of me getting fucked at Hickford Park to that new Hickford Homo website. Right now it seemed that few people knew of the new website's existence, but it would only be a matter of time before word spread about town, and I really did not like the idea of being one of its stars. It was one thing me being aware of my Hickford Homo status...but all of Moa Hill?

No thanks.

I'm not sure if it was the pot, or my lowly status as a faggot, but the Savage boys basically ignored my existence while I sat right in front of them. Instead of talking to me, they talked *about* me:

"The thing about fags," Darren said, "is that they know how to suck cock, and they love sucking cock. That's the thing most guys don't realise. A faggot is always grateful for a feed. Always."

"Fully, bro," Jockey agreed.

"You could probably even feed a faggot piss straight from your cock for breakfast and it would say thank you," Darren said, with the grin of someone about to cause trouble. "There's just something about the way their brains are wired...they just love anything to do with alpha dick."

Jockey nodded, looking like he was giving that some serious thought.

"I gotta say I'm a bit jealous you got yourself such a pretty one," Darren said, his drunken gaze drifting over me. "With that long blond hair you could fuck him from behind and just pretend he's a chick."

"I think I'd have to make Mike wax his ass crack for that fantasy to feel real."

They both laughed at my expense. I didn't mind. I was too busy entertaining a fantasy of my own: the two of them together.

My taboo daydream was fuelled by the homoerotic sight of their naked shoulders touching, and the relaxed way Jockey's knee rested against his brother's outstretched legs. Adding to my twisted fantasy was the story Jockey had told me about how he and Darren used to suck each other off after school. Even though I didn't have the slightest spark of interest in Darren, not really, I could not deny that the image of these two Savage boys noshing one another off turned me on.

Jockey had the better body of the two; in no small part thanks to his job as a labourer. My master's abs were more visible than his older brother's and his treasure trail thicker, darker. Darren didn't quite have abs: he had ribs, and a thin shield of muscle, and nothing much else but badly-drawn tattoos.

I wonder if Darren is the big brother in more ways than one...

As if he had sensed my silent question, Darren adjusted his crotch. I think he caught me licking my lips, because he sat there with a satisfied grin on his face.

"Tell me, Mike... what made you decide to give my numbnuts little brother ownership of your pussy?" Darren asked. "A good-looking guy like you could pretty much have his pick of men who are into that sort of thing."

The crass compliment made me feel good but I could see Jockey fidgeting. My master was annoyed at Darren's not-so subtle dig, but I knew he wouldn't say anything. While the rest of the world viewed his older siblings as the dumb, tatted-up trashy white thugs that they were, Jockey had always idolised his brothers, and rarely called them out when they bullied or ridiculed him.

Well, not on my watch.

"I signed the contract because I don't think anyone will ever be capable of fucking me the way Jockey does."

"Is that so?" Darren said facetiously. He wasn't quite grinning anymore.

"It is. I never thought of myself as a submissive person until the night Jockey fucked me. But now I can't stop thinking about his big dick and how good it makes me feel."

"You hear that, Jocks?" Darren nudged his brother with a thin, sinewy arm. "Mike here reckons you've got a big dick."

Jockey nodded again, totally disinterested.

"Does Jockey make you squeal like a bitch, does he, brah?" Darren asked me excitedly. "Gives it to you nice 'n good 'n deep?"

"He does."

"Jocks is definitely gonna make you squeal when he gets around to fisting you. He's told me that's part of your contract. You do understand that he's totally gonna leave you with a bucket ass by the time he's finished with you, right?"

"And I will be proud he was the man who did it to me."

Darren chuckled, a short, barking, contemptuous sound. "You say that but something tells me you're the sort of faggot who would be proud to let any man fuck your cunt."

"Not any man," I said, daring to take a dig I knew I shouldn't. "I prefer to be fucked by men who have never taken a cock up their ass."

Darren's jaw ticked. "Why's that?"

"Because then I know I'm being fucked by an alpha male, not another bitch."

Jockey finally cracked a smile, but I could see Darren's eyes glowing with an unspoken rage. I had hit a nerve.

"Mike's right," Jockey said. "Alpha men are the best fucks. And a man can't be an alpha male if he's been deflowered...like a bitch."

I didn't believe a word of this alpha bullshit but I nodded along like I did; purely to watch Darren sweat a little as he tried his best to act natural. It seemed that Jockey didn't know his brother's secret—that he'd been raped in prison—but I knew.

Darren drained the beer he was drinking, belched in my direction, then told Jockey he was heading inside to the main house.

"Thank you," Jockey said when his brother was gone.

"For what?"

"For showing me respect in front of my brother. And for talking me up."

"I didn't say anything that wasn't true."

"I guess you didn't but it never hurts for other alphas like Daz to know these things."

Alphas like Daz my ass. I was tempted to say something, but I thought better of it. Still, that didn't stop me saying something else entirely inappropriate: "I thought Darren of all people would know how big your dick is, considering he used to suck it all the time."

Jockey laughed. "That spins your wheels that, doesn't it? Thinking of me and Daz together like that?"

"No."

"Be honest, bitch. You should know better than to lie to me."

"Well...maybe I do find it a little hot. There's something transgressive about it that I like."

"What are you on about?" Jockey looked confused. "We aren't angry trannies."

Lord give me strength. "What I mean is there's something a bit naughty about it. Like you two crossed a line brothers shouldn't, and that's what makes it so hot."

"I s'pose that makes sense." A crude smile followed. "Who knows? Maybe one day I'll ask Daz if he wants to reenact the scene so you can watch. But only if you're a good boy."

My dick punched against my jeans. I had never wanted to be a good boy so much in my life. And I decided that the first act of being a good boy was to give Jockey the consent form Trent had filled in. I dug into my pocket and pulled out the green form and handed it over. "This is for you, sir." I reached into my pocket again and slid out the slimy sperm-filled rubber that had been buried in my asshole little more than an hour ago. "And this."

Jockey's eyes lit up at the sight of the rubber. He held it up high to the sunlight streaming through the window, inspecting it as if it were a work of art. "The man can shoot decent loads," he remarked.

"Yeah. He can."

Jockey let the condom slop onto the couch beside him and began to read over the accompanying consent form. I waited for a lecture about the broken condom. But to my surprise, and relief, Jockey was all smiles when he finished reading the form.

"Well done," he said. "This is how it should be."

"Really?"

"Yes. You followed an order *and* made sure the guy filled out the form. I'm impressed."

"Impressed enough to let me watch you and Darren?"

He laughed. "No, sorry. Daz and I ain't sucked each other off for years so you'll have to work harder to see that happen."

"What about just letting me suck your cock instead?" I reached out and stroked the top of his barefoot. "I can swallow your load for you if that's what you'd like?"

"No, Mike." He shook my hand away from his foot. "I've told you we are waiting until Monday."

First Trent and now you!

The reality was both men's rejections were for very different reasons, and arguably Jockey's decline to let me suck his cock wasn't technically even a rejection. If anything he was being sensible, like a parent not allowing their child to open any of their Christmas presents early. But I was feeling fragile damn it, and I wanted access to my master's goodies.

A bratty sulk right now felt like a good option, but instead I resorted to weaponizing my sex appeal; or what I assumed was my sex appeal.

While Jockey reverted to a zombie-like state, sat there in a stoner daze, I proceeded to take my shoes and socks off. When he

131

didn't say anything, I stretched my legs and scrunched my toes on the grubby carpet, trying my best to look natural.

He started laughing. "You're not as subtle as you think you are, bitch."

"What do you mean?" I said, playing dumb.

"Showing off your feet like that. You know how much they turn me on." His eyes gave me a quick up-and-down. They stuck on something. Something in my pocket. "What's that?" he asked.

I glanced down and saw a bit of paper poking out of my pocket. "That's the note you gave me at the park yesterday."

As if he didn't believe me, Jockey snatched it from my pocket and began to read it aloud. That's when I realised *his* note was in my other pocket.

"*I am housesitting for a friend in town at 228 Carrington Street. I would love it if you popped around after work tonight to keep me company...*" Jockey's voice went quiet as he read the rest of the note in silence before staring at me in disbelief. "So where's the cash? I'm assuming this is the same guy who filled in the consent form."

"No. God no. The note is from someone else."

"Who?"

"Just some old guy who came into the bar."

"Can you be any more specific?"

I could but I don't want to. "There's not much else to say. He was old, and apparently rich."

"I guess the details aren't important," Jockey said. "Especially when there's that much money to be made."

"You're not suggesting I should have gone through with it, are you?"

"I'm not *suggesting* it, I'm saying it. When a man offers you that sort of money you give him what he wants."

"But eww."

"There is nothing eww about a thousand dollars, Mike."

"There is if I have to suck grey balls to get it."

Jockey sighed and gave me an exaggerated eyeroll. "Yeah well, sometimes in life we just have to take one for the team."

"That doesn't sound very alpha male of you."

That got at least a quirk of his lip, almost a smile. "I'm not talking about me, smart ass. I'm talking about you. Alphas don't suck dick for cash. That's the domain of faggots and substandard betas."

"But I don't want to be a whore."

"What's it matter? It doesn't change what you are."

"I think you'll find it does."

"You need to stop fighting this sort of thing and just accept your true nature. You're a faggot. And faggots are supposed to be slutty. It's what Darren was talking about earlier."

"Don't you think that's a bit offensive to label all gay men as promiscuous?"

"I'm not talking about gay men. I'm talking about guys like you. Faggots. They don't have any self-respect when it comes to cock."

I wasn't sure about that claim of no self-respect, but then again, I had woken up this morning leaking semen out my ass onto the bedsheets of a married man. So...

"I'm guessing you haven't been doing your homework. Because if you had then I wouldn't have to be educating you about yourself. I gave you those websites to look up. The Hierarchy should tell you all about it."

"The hierarchy," I repeated.

"You need to learn all this stuff, Mike. It's only by knowing who you are, and embracing it, that you can reach your full potential. And by doing that you will help me reach mine."

"Why are you so obsessed with this hierarchy stuff anyway? Isn't it enough that I've signed a contract and agreed to do what you ask?"

I expected a sharp rebuke, but that's not what I got.

"Because hierarchy is truth," he said. "Every fucker we know is a liar. The government. Our families. The people we think are our friends, like fuckface Brian. They all talk shit. They all want us to think that they're kind and have our best interest at heart. But they don't. Very few people are actually kind. But hierarchy... it's the one thing you can be sure of. And to me that's a form of kindness I can believe in. It lets you know your place in the world, and your place is here with me, at my feet."

I don't think he had ever sounded more insane or looked more beautiful to me than in this moment. Jockey Savage may have only been twenty-one but already he knew that he didn't care for the world as it was. He couldn't change this one, so he had built his own. And it was a world he wanted me to be a part of.

I bent down, kowtowing before him, and pressed my lips to the sinewy surface of the top of his foot. I exhaled slowly, stirring a few light hairs between his toe-knuckles.

"What are you doing, bitch?" he asked.

"Honouring you, sir." I licked between his long toes. He wiggled them. I cupped the back of his ankles and pulled my face in tight against his foot; worshipping, honouring, submitting.

But I was doing more than worshipping, honouring and submitting. I was showing Jockey that I understood. I understood his resentment. I understood what he was searching for. I understood what he wanted out of his new world. But most of all I understood that it was a world where I too could belong.

Chapter 13

"I REALLY FUCKED UP."

That was the first thing Gavin said to me as I walked in the house after visiting Jockey. He was sitting at the dining table, tilted back in the chair, staring into space. One leg of his grey sweatpants was halfway up his shin, baring a stretch of silken-hairy leg.

"What's happened?" I asked, standing at the kitchen bench.

He took a deep breath and let it out slowly, puffing out his cheeks. "There's good news and bad news."

I braced myself for something like this: *Good news is I'm getting married. Bad news is your ass has to move out.*

"Hit me with the bad news first," I said.

"You know how I told you about Fiona telling me she loved me?"

"Yeah?"

"It turns out that's not what she said. Apparently she said '*I luff you*' to be cute."

"Oh..." I could see where this was going and I had to do my best not to smile in relief.

"So you can imagine her fucking surprise when she turned up today earlier than I had anticipated and saw that cunting thing on the table."

I had been so distracted by the man's hairy calf muscle on display that I hadn't even noticed *that cunting thing*. It was a brochure Gavin had picked up yesterday from a jewellery store; bride and groom on the front. Not very subtle.

Cringing inwardly, I asked, "What did she say when she saw it?"

"After demanding to know why I had a brochure about engagement rings, and me telling her the truth, she laughed her fucking ass off."

"Ouch."

"Ouch indeed." He lowered the chair down and chuckled to himself. "The truth is I am a bit relieved. I'm not the sort of guy who likes to rush these things."

"Then why did you?"

"That's the good news," he said. "Fiona reckons it's cause of the chastity cage I've been wearing. Said it has a tendency to make some men a bit more gushy than normal. And I've certainly been feeling pretty fucking gushy lately."

"Or maybe you haven't been getting enough sleep. Lack of sleep fucks with your brain."

"Come to think of it, I have been tired a lot lately." He glanced over at me. "How did you know?"

"Two words: nocturnal erections. You're bound to have broken sleeps if you're going to bed wearing a chastity cage. Each time your dick wants to go for a midnight stroll it's gonna wake you up, probably sore."

He hooked his hands behind his head and gazed at me. "You seem rather knowledgeable on this topic, young Mikey. Is there something you haven't been telling me?"

"No. It's just commonsense." The lie felt thin coming out of my mouth, and I worried he could see right through it.

He pondered that for a moment before eventually agreeing with me. "I suppose it is."

"Anyway, you still haven't actually told me *why* this is good news."

"Because..." Gavin sprung to his feet then turned to face me. His hands reached for the front of his sweatpants and lowered them, just enough to give me a full shot of black pubes and a sneaky peek at the base of his naked dick. "She's let me take it off! Isn't that awesome?"

All too soon those grey sweatpants were resting back on his hips, ending five of the best seconds of my life. I just stared at him, stupidly.

"I have not jerked off so many times in one day since I was fourteen," Gavin said. "And that's even after Fiona and I had ourselves some fun. I've even enjoyed just going for a piss. Man, I missed standing up to pee."

Now that I knew the cage was gone, I couldn't stop flicking discreet glances at his crotch.

"What about the threesome?" I asked. "I thought she said you had to wear the cage until that happens."

"We've agreed to put that on hold for a while. Thank fuck."

"So you admit now you were letting Fiona push you outside of your comfort zone?" I had my preachy face on to match my preachy tone.

He leaned back, steepling his fingers. He didn't speak to begin with, just regarded me thoughtfully.

Finally, he said, "I wouldn't say that. I was just a bit apprehensive about the anal side of things. I don't know how you do it. Just thinking about a cock going inside such a tiny hole makes my eyes water."

Suddenly all I could feel was the burn in my asshole from the pounding Trent had given me.

"Sorry," Gavin said. "That's a bit insensitive of me to just assume that's what you do."

"That's okay. You're probably still getting used to having blood running through your main brain again."

"But you do that, right? Take it up the—"

"What I do is not have conversations like these."

"Don't be such a prude. It's me you're talking to." He grinned, and then the grin dissolved into a smile. "The man you once thought was a bit of alright."

I still do, I wanted to say.

When I failed to respond, he got up and joined me in the kitchen and filled up the kettle. "Fancy a hot chocolate?" he asked.

"Not for me, thanks."

He fossicked through the dirty dishes on the bench, looking for the cleanest cup he could find. It was his turn to do the washing up—had been for days—but he still hadn't gotten around to it.

Gavin suddenly leaned close enough for me to feel his warm breath against my ear. Then, he sniffed me. "You smell nice," he drawled, his voice a velvet-on-gravel purr.

"Do I?"

"Yeah." He took another whiff, just above my collarbone. "I'm not sure but I think Trent might use the same cologne."

Trent's cologne had probably rubbed off on me, but I was pretty sure my body would have reeked more of the man's sweat and semen. Fearing Gavin might have been a sniffer dog in a past life, I stepped around him and made my way to my room.

Sitting down on my bed, I plugged my phone in to charge and then kicked off my shoes. I glanced over at my laptop sat on my desk, wondering if I should have a go at working on my novel for a couple hours. Instead, I opted to do some research on the hierarchy.

I wouldn't say I was overly enthused to learn about Jockey's sexual belief system, but I also knew that if I wanted to stop crushing on Gavin then I had to throw myself into my new role as Jockey's faggot. It would be the perfect distraction, I thought, to become lost in Jockey's kinky world.

After navigating my way towards the hierarchy website I was once again taken aback by the amount of articles and videos on offer. The site was a treasure trove of depraved information with an emphasis on the power pyramid of men. Picture after picture, video after video, showed alpha males using faggots. The most common pictures were faggots who'd just endured a thorough breeding; hunched over, ass aimed at the camera, their cum-filled holes declaring to the world what they were. What I was...

For the most part what I read blurred into mindless drivel, and I struggled to stay focused, until a particular article caught my attention. It was to do with something I had heard Jockey and Damian talk about. It was an article titled: The Magic of Cunting.

CUNTING IS A PHYSIOLOGICAL condition within a faggot caused by the stimulation/penetration of the faggot's second ring. This produces dramatic euphoria, and a neverending need to be fucked. This changes the faggot forever. They no longer seek their own pleasure. Their assholes become their true sex organ.

When a Man cunts a faggot, he exerts his power over them and unlocks the submissiveness they have buried beneath years of ego and illusions. Once a faggot has been cunted, there is simply no way for them to reclaim their manhood. The cunting utterly destroys that possibility permanently.

THE MORE I READ THE more questions I had. Was there really such a thing? Could a man be fucked so hard, and so deeply, that it could change him sexually? I'd heard of what Gavin had jokingly referred to as a 'bum cum'—orgasm through stimulation of the prostate—but this... this sounded different.

It also sounded fucking ridiculous!

I don't think most Men understand the true power of their cocks. It isn't just a piece of flesh that ejaculates. It is the tool a Man uses to claim what is his, the blunt instrument of his masculine power. When he penetrates an inferior, he owns them body and soul.

Cunting is the end result of a Man's use of his cock in the act of rutting, of dominating. Some scholars in this field may disagree with my next observation but in my experience not all Men are capable of cunting a faggot, and not all faggots can be cunted. This does not diminish their respective roles but it does point to there being a hierarchy amongst each side. Only the most alpha of Men will be able to unlock this power and only the truly inferior of submissives can accept this incredibly freeing and terrifying gift.

THE SANE, RATIONAL part of my brain was keen to dismiss these ramblings as the words of an oversexed porn addict, but on some level I found myself open to believing what was being said. Maybe it was because I knew firsthand the power of penetration. Once a man had his dick inside your ass then you were at the mercy of his hips and intentions. And sure, depending on the man, and the situation, it could be emasculating.

Even so this article is full of shit, I told myself.

And the more I thought about it, the more it bugged me. The internet was already rife with crazy conspiracy theories and misinformation so it wasn't like it needed any more. And it certainly didn't need crazy sex tales parading online as facts that could give impressionable men like Jockey warped ideas. If Jockey wanted to live in his own fantasy world, fine. But it needed to be tethered to at least some semblance of reality.

Feeling like my old self again—an opinionated know-it-all—I began to typing in the comment section to tell the author of the article that they didn't know what they were talking about. Unfortunately a quiet knock at my bedroom door forced me to abandon the post.

"Yeah?" I called out, quickly closing my laptop.

Gavin opened the door and came in. "What do you fancy for dinner? I thought I could go to the shops for some junk food for a movie night and pick up dinner while I am there?"

"Anyone would think this is a special occasion," I said.

"It is a special occasion. I'm a free man again, remember?"

While Gavin laughed at his own joke, I stole another glance at the bulge in his pants.

"I'll just take a shower first," said Gavin, unbuttoning his shirt and splitting it into halves, shrugging it over his shoulders and off. He stood naked from the waist up, totally unaware the effect he was having on me.

A sensation rolled up my body, prickling my skin. It might have been shame or lust, or maybe some mixture of both. My cock stirred against my boxers and jeans, and I dropped a hand over my lap to hide my arousal fuelled by an onslaught of improper thoughts.

Stop being an idiot, I told myself. *He's your stepfather, not someone you can fantasise about.*

But it was hard not to fantasise about Gavin when he turned away from me and I saw those broad shoulders tapering down to his narrow waist. This wasn't helped by the thin fabric of his sweatpants clinging in the cleft of his ass, outlining its firm roundness. He had an ass a man his age should be proud of. The sort of ass I'd love to get up close and personal with.

Instead of my inner voice scolding me again for entertaining such incestuous thoughts, it was Jockey's voice and words echoing in my mind.

Faggots don't have any self-respect when it comes to cock.

Chapter 14

EVERY TOWN HAS A SEEDY underbelly. And Moa Hill was no exception.

I'd known this ever since I was a child when I'd eavesdrop to my mother's work stories about her job as a barmaid at one of Moa Hill's shadier taverns. That was how I knew that more often than not a house fire in my neighbourhood wasn't someone being careless and leaving the oven on, it was someone being careless and not paying a drug debt. These work stories were also how I knew that an old villa around the corner from our house was actually a brothel, not the family home of a crusty old Pakeha and his Filipino wife and lovely daughters. Despite knowing these things I was still shocked to discover my provincial backwater town had a gay sex club.

I had learned this latest salacious piece of information after spending most of the morning locked in my bedroom researching the websites Jockey had told me to look up. I'd started by reading up more on the Hierarchy where I found an in-depth article explaining to alphas the importance of breeding their faggots regularly. Again, it was all cockamamie bullshit but the rather unscientific claims were quite entertaining, and I could see how some men would go along with it.

Things like: *When a Man pumps his load into a faggot, the semen enters the faggot's bloodstream and the powerful chemicals in the semen are assimilated into the faggot's body. This has the effect of altering the faggot's brain chemistry and causes the faggot to become more submissive.*

So while such dirty gems had me torn between chuckling and catching myself nodding in submissive agreement, it wasn't this article, or even the corresponding website, that had alluded me to the fact Moa Hill had a sex club for men thirsting for the D.

That I found on the website hosting the Hickford Homo videos.

It turned out there were way more videos on that site than I had realised. Quite often it was the same faces appearing in them but all up there must have been at least thirty different men who had found themselves unlucky enough to be caught on camera. It wasn't until I'd gotten to the last page of the videos that I saw at the bottom a small advertisement for something called The Factory.

If you are looking for man-on-man fun that won't ruin your reputation like these poor cunts in the videos then make sure you start attending party nights here at The Factory. We provide a safe place to fuck and suck without the risk of being caught with your pants down. For more information on how to get an invite to one of our party nights then get in touch.

Below was a mobile number and email address, along with a line in even smaller font explaining that there was a charge to attend the parties. My first thought was *why not just open a gay bar?* But then I realised this factory place wasn't about a night out with drinks. It was purely to get down and dirty like the men did in Hickford Park. A sort of safe space for cruising.

145

The old prude in me thought it was kind of gross. The horny nineteen-year-old in me thought it was clever, and perhaps even useful. Had I known about its existence sooner I maybe could have avoided earning myself the Hickford Homo label.

While I'd found the existence of such a club in Moa Hill a bit shocking, it paled in comparison to the shock I had gotten from watching more of the Hickford Homo videos. I hadn't watched them all but I'd seen enough to decide that the one with Isaac Fraser and that skinhead dude called Moose was my favourite. I think what made it so hot was the way Isaac sounded like a bitch on heat; animalistic moans and groans coming from the school boy's lips as a man probably twice his age pummelled Isaac's anal cavity with a cock that was big enough to be considered a weapon of mass destruction.

And I must admit there was a dark thrill in listening to Isaac being made say "*Loose by Moose. Loose by Moose. Loose by Moose*" over and over.

Gavin had gone out for brunch with Fiona which meant I was able to have the volume up loud and really appreciate the desperately sexy sounds coming through my laptop's speakers. I had not known Isaac particularly well at school. To be honest, before his infamy at winding up online as a Hickford Homo he'd been little more than a face in the crowd to me. A popular face for sure, but still just a face. However, I knew his speaking voice was nothing like the bitch-whimpers being fucked out of him on my screen right now. If anything was going to make me believe in a hierarchy made up of alphas and faggots then it was a video like this.

With my pants and boxers pooled at my ankles, I was halfway through watching the video for the fifth time in a row when my phone interrupted with a call from Jockey.

146

"H-Hello," I spluttered, trying my best not to sound like I was in the middle of a wank.

"Hey bitch," Jockey said curtly. "Are you busy right now?"

I glanced down at my erection and then at my laptop screen paused on a closeup shot of Isaac's cock-stuffed asshole. "Uh... only a little busy."

"Then don't be. I need you to go to my aunt and uncle's house and mow the lawns."

"What? You want me to mow lawns?"

"They needed to be mown days ago but I was hoping to leave them until your contract starts. Figured I'd just get you to do them and save myself a job. But my aunt and uncle had a fucking bitch fit about them this morning before I left for work, so I told them I'd get them done today."

My mind was spinning. It hadn't occurred to me that being Jockeys faggot would involve physical labour.

"Are you there, bitch?"

"I'm here." I took a breath. "So mowing *your* lawns is part of my responsibilities?"

He could sense I was annoyed. "That shouldn't come as a surprise. You'll be doing my housework too. One of the main reasons a man owns a faggot is to make his life easier. And you'll make mine plenty easier if you help out with chores now and then. Mowing lawns once a week or two isn't going to kill you."

"I know that I just..."

"You just?"

"Nothing."

The line went quiet.

When Jockey finally spoke, his voice was low and calm, and somehow all the more menacing for that. "So can you head around

147

and do them today? Or do I have to call my uncle and tell him you'll come and do them Monday?"

"Why Monday?"

"Because you can't tell me no then."

"I see..."

"But it'll be easier on you if you get them done today. With this weather we're having who knows how fast they'll grow over the next three days."

He had a point, and it was one that made my erection soften. Hard work had never been a turn-on for me.

"Fine," I said, feeling weighted down with second thoughts about this contract. "Let me get changed and then I'll come mow them."

"Cheers, bitch. And feel free to leave me a tribute before you leave."

"A tribute?"

"Yeah. Your cum. My sleepout's unlocked so you can go in and jizz over my pillow or something. It'd be nice to have something tasty to lick up when I get home from work."

And just like that my second thoughts were replaced with visions of a bright and horny future.

Chapter 15

SUMMER'S SWEET-SMELLING breeze caressed my face but its humid kisses did little to cool me down. When I had left my house over an hour ago, I had been riding the high of Jockey's sexy desire to lick up my cum. Now though, pushing a lawnmower around a lawn that felt like the size of an Olympic swimming pool and made of quicksand, the only thing I was riding was a chafed asshole.

Note to self: next time you mow these fucking lawns make sure you do it when it isn't ball-sweat o'clock!

I had already ditched my singlet but that had done little to cool me down. I was feeling overheated and dehydrated, and I could detect the start of sunburn manifesting itself on the skin of my arms, back and neck. My penchant for always wearing jeans wasn't helping matters either. The denim material felt like leeches stuck to my slick and slimy legs, and I was tempted to whip them off and finish the lawns in just my boxers.

More than once I contemplated abandoning the lawns halfway through, but I knew that wasn't an option. Not unless I wanted a good ear bollocking over the phone from Jockey when he got home from work. The other thing holding me hostage to this ass-chafing, ball-sweating labour—and the reason I hadn't taken off my jeans—was Jockey's uncle who sat in the comfort of his airconditioned lounge and was watching me like a hawk through the open ranch slider.

I now regretted paying Jockey his "tribute" before mowing the lawns. It was as if half my energy had shot out of my cock, landing on Jockey's pillow with three wet splats. Still, I couldn't help but smile knowing that my master would be coming home from work to lick up my spunk. It was crazy as fuck but so dam sexy, and fun, and hot, and oh so Jockey.

Just as I was nearly finished mowing, Mr Savage swaggered his way out onto the patio. The man was dressed in his best white trash fashion: a sauce-stained white wifebeater over his lean torso, long legs clad in grey sweatpants and his big socked-feet fitted with a pair of lime-green Crocs. He stood with his feet apart and arms akimbo. It was such an arrogant pose, like he was supervising me at work.

If you want it mown better then maybe you should mow it yourself, asshole.

It wasn't like his unemployed ass didn't have the time. While his wife Jocelynn worked fifty hour weeks, busting her ass as a commercial cleaner, this lazy turd spent all day at home on the couch drinking beer and chain-smoking. To Jockey and his brothers he was known as Uncle Chris but to most people in town Chris Savage was known by the moniker of Stretch. The nickname was appropriate considering he was six-foot-four, towering above most people wherever he went. Despite being so tall he wasn't what I'd call physically intimidating; his lanky legs and noodle arms didn't appear to have much strength.

When I'd mown over the last of the long grass, I went and emptied the catcher into the compost heap and was about to put the lawnmower away in the shed when Stretch waved me over.

I approached the tall git with a smile. "Hi, Stretch."

He didn't reply straight away. Instead, he stood there like a statue surveying the freshly mown lawn.

Up close you could see traces of what had once been a handsome face. In his youth, Chris Savage would have been better looking than any of his nephews, but age and decades of heavy drinking and smoking had taken its toll. His scowling face was gaunt and his teeth stained from a pack-a-day habit that had also yellowed the tips of two of his fingers. The dispassion in his steady, golden eyes made me think the man was incapable of flashing a kind smile.

Done with scrutinizing my hard work, his gaze took a tour along my sweat-soaked clothes as he drifted closer, so close I detected fumes of beer on his breath. The piney, masculine aroma reminded me of his nephew, agitating my hunger and stirred other things I refused to acknowledge.

I met his eyes. "Does the lawn get the seal of approval?"

"I guess so," he huffed before aiming a finger in the far corner of the yard. "But you did fuck up a bit down near the fence. You can't just zig and zag a lawn. It's gotta be done properly."

I didn't bother turning around to look where he was pointing.

Running a hand through his thinning brown hair, he said, "Did Jockey tell you that I wanted to have a chat with you?"

"No. He didn't mention that."

"Oh well. Go put the mower away then come inside and join me for a beer. You and I need to have a chat."

I didn't want to join this man for anything, but I also didn't want to be rude. I also wasn't about to turn down whatever money he was about to give me for mowing the lawns, which I assumed was what he wanted to talk about.

When I joined Stretch in the lounge he was already sat down on the couch, a can of beer between his legs like he was using it to cool down his balls.

"If you fancy a beer then grab one from the fridge," he said.

My mouth was crying out for a cold drink, but I declined, not wanting to spend a second longer in this man's company than I absolutely had to. Ever since Jockey had told me about how his uncle used to beat him as a kid, I'd not liked this asshole, and a free beer on a hot day wasn't going to change that.

I took a seat on a tattered armchair off to the side, just far enough away not to smell the stink coming from the overflowing ashtray on the coffee table. Stretch didn't say anything, just looked at me like I was an inconvenience, which was odd considering he'd been the one to invite me inside.

"What did you want to talk with me about?" I asked, looking around for any sign of his wallet.

"Is Jockey porking you?"

The question took me by surprise and left me speechless. I mean...who the fuck asks that sort of question? And what the fuck do you say to that?

"It's an easy question, son. Is Jockey sticking his diddle in ya shitbox or not?"

My inner submissive answered for me: "Yes, sir. He is."

I waited for Jockey's uncle to laugh and mock me, but that's not what he did. He just nodded thoughtfully, albeit judgementally.

"I'm not surprised," he muttered. "You look the type."

Well, fuck you too, I thought.

"I've known for years the sorts of games that Jockey likes to play. Him and Darren didn't think their aunty and I could hear them while they were growing up. But we could. But what can you

152

do? As I explained to Jocelynn these are the sorts of games boys of a certain age like to play. But I thought Jockey might have grown out of that sort of silly business by now."

"I don't think you can say someone's sexuality is silly business."

He rolled his eyes. "Don't give me any of that awake nonsense."

"Do you mean woke?"

"Fuck knows what it's called. All that PC bullshit we get on our televisions these days with dudes wanting to wear dresses and be called mam."

Someone looks like they're winning bigot of the year.

"That sort of thing has been happening since Christ was a cowboy," Stretch said. "Who gives a shit? I know I don't. Do what makes you happy I say. But that don't mean I need to hear some fuckwit from Ponsonby on the television tell me what a piece of shit I am for not wanting to suck a crossdresser's cock."

On second thoughts he probably won't win the award. Just get nominated.

I thought he was done with his redneck musing but he continued talking. "I don't know what it is about my nephews. All three of them think too much with their peckers. At least Jockey ain't a thief like the other two, but even so he ain't exactly what I'd describe as well-adjusted. You see all that army shit he wears? The lad's a little special."

I had reached the point where I couldn't not say anything to this asshole. "Maybe if you treated Jockey and his brothers better growing up you'd have less to whinge about."

"What's that supposed to mean?"

"It means you don't beat children to the point they're black and blue or wind up with a broken arm." I shot him the most lethal glare I could summon, letting him know he didn't intimidate me.

I half-expected a fight, or at the very least told to get out of his house. But all he did was laugh.

When Stretch finally stopped laughing he made a sombre sounding tsk-tsk. "Jockey tell you that, did he?"

"Yes. And I saw the bruises."

"He's telling you porkies, mate. I've never laid a hand on any of my nephews. Maybe if I had then the little fuckers wouldn't keep finding themselves in trouble with the pigs."

"But Jockey used to come to school with bruises all the time."

"Don't I fucking know it." He laughed again before slurping back a mouthful of beer, several dribbles sliding down his chin and landing onto the already stained wifebeater. "I was called into the principal's office more than once to rebuke those tall tales."

"They weren't tall tales!"

He dismissed my tinny-sounding outrage with a snort. "You're an only child, ain't that right, son?"

"Yeah. So?"

"So I don't think you realise just how fucking brutal siblings can be. Jockey was the runt of the litter, the youngest and the tiniest, but he had the smartest mouth on him. Meanwhile he had two older brothers more than happy to keep his mouthy lip in line. Well...that was until he was just as big as them and able to fight back. Then they were all walking around with bruises and the occasional bloody nose. Don't get me wrong, those boys would do anything for each other, but that don't mean they can't fight like two fat slags after the last cream donut in the cabinet."

It made sense. But...

Jockey's not a liar.

Stretch smiled smugly. He could tell I was doubting myself. He then added, "Did you ever stop to think that maybe Jockey told you stories to try and impress you? Maybe shock you? Maybe get your attention? Your sympathy?"

I wanted to argue, but I found myself hesitating. Why? Because that's exactly the sort of thing Jockey was known to do. To paint a story larger and crazier than it was in reality. Yet despite Jockey's tendency to embellish the truth, I had always considered him one of the most honest people I know, especially about the things that mattered. Things he had told me in private. But could Jockey's trait to exaggerate extend itself to him playing the victim for attention? I hoped not because if that were the case then I would owe this man an apology for thinking the worst of him for years now.

Fuck...

Stretch licked a stray drip of beer from his index finger. "My brother Marcus, Jockey's father, he was a nice guy. A bit dull but very normal. The crazy comes from the boys' mother's side. Sarah was a lovely-looking woman with an ass to die for, but she was nuttier than squirrel shit. She had a big heart, cared a lot about the people she loved, but could also be a cunning bitch." Stretch paused for a moment, smiling like he was remembering fond memories. "Jockey's the most like her of the three boys. Which probably explains why he's always been my favourite. A cheeky fucker with a heart of gold just like his mum. Sarah was always good for a laugh. She didn't give a toss what people thought of her. I always admired that. And fuck was she was clever. Much cleverer than people gave her credit for. That's very Jockey."

"Jockey's smart?" I didn't mean it to sound like a question.

"Of course he's bloody smart," Stretch said with a chuckle. "Why else do you think you've spent the last hour out there sweating your nuts off mowing my lawns."

"Fair point."

"Which brings me to what I wanted to speak with you about. Jockey tells me you and him have come to an arrangement of sorts. A sort of queer sex thing. That right?"

For fuck's sake, Jockey! It was bad enough he'd told his brother but his uncle too... what the hell was wrong with this family?

"That's right," I mumbled, my face burning hot with shame.

"You're the one taking it up the shitter, am I correct?"

"I really don't see how that's relevant."

"I'll take that as a yes," he said, smirking like an asshole.

"You can take it however you want but it still isn't relevant."

"I suppose not," he conceded and drained the last of his beer. "Anyway, what Jockey chooses to do in the privacy of his sleepout is his business. Provided you two don't wake the neighbours up with your butt fucking then I don't care how much he roots you."

"That's very kind of you."

"You're welcome," Stretch replied, too dense to sense my sarcasm. "And if I'm being honest then I'd rather he be nutting in you than some dopey bitch who he could get knocked up. The last thing Jocelyn and I want is to raise someone else's kids again. We've been there done that, bought the t-shirt. But I'm also aware that this arrangement you lads have means you'll be staying over here quite a lot, so I just wanted to let you know that it would be good of you to perhaps throw me some money each week to offset some of them extra costs with the power and whatnot."

So that was it. That is what he wanted to talk about. Me giving him money. Not the other way around.

"I will be sure to pay my way," I said before telling him I had to get going home. I'd had enough embarrassment for one day.

Just as I was about to walk outside, Stretch said to me, "I hope you know what you're doing, Mike. Jockey's a good egg but he's a very broken boy."

I pretended I hadn't heard him and walked out the door with the shiver of an unwanted truth running down my spine.

Chapter 16

RAIN LASHED THE MOA Hill event centre on what had unexpectedly turned into a stormy Saturday night. The thick, clotted drops clung to the outside of the misted-over windows, reminding me of sweat. The illusion was no doubt brought on by my own sweatiness. I'd had to walk here in the early evening heat, running the last few blocks before the skies opened up with a downpour. Now I was sat at a table with my work colleagues, praying my deodorant could mask my natural scent.

Due to my mind focusing on other matters—my impending servitude to Jockey and my resurging Gavin crush—I had totally forgotten that the Moa Hill Hospitality Awards were on tonight. The awards only occurred once every two years and were considered a big deal in the town, which is why the local event centre was packed not just with bar owners and their underpaid staff but also with an array of the town's social elite.

To be invited by your boss was a bit of an honour, so I was told, but quite honestly I would have preferred to be back at the bar working. At least then I'd be getting paid to be bored shitless. I'd secretly hoped that my choice of outfit would have had me refused entry at the door, but for some reason the ticket clerk hardly gave me a second look. The outfit in question was what I called my "combat rock" look: black t-shirt with an "A" for anarchy emblazoned in pink on the back; tight, black jeans with frayed cuffs; and decrepit sneakers.

Much to my boss Carol's disappointment, our little café/bar was only up for one award—bartender of the year. So while Carol was salty about Chaos being overlooked, her hipster son was floating on cloud nine at being nominated for his cocktail talents. Chad didn't end up winning but that didn't stop him celebrating like he had when the award portion of the night ended and we all made our way into the adjoining bar.

During the evening our work group become friendly with the crew from The Rusty Nail—a bar just a few shops down from Chaos. Similar to us, they had only been nominated for one award so we bonded in neglect from the industry. One of the barmen from the Rusty Nail was a guy from my neighbourhood and who I had gone to school with: Brigham Moss. We had been in a couple classes together at high school, chatted on occasion, but had never been what you'd call friends.

With a name like Brigham it shouldn't come as a surprise to hear that his family were devout Mormons. But while Brigham's parents and siblings were all very much followers of the Utah religion—keeping away from coffee and tea, and I assumed wore those magic undies I'd heard about—Brigham was the black sheep of his family on account of falling victim (or free depending on how you look at it) to the vices of the world. He smoked, drank and dabbled with pot like most guys our age.

Semi-cute with his short, dark hair and facial scruff—which I figured owed more to a slacker's laziness than a serious attempt to grow a true goatee and moustache—and feet that looked too big for the rest of him, Brigham moaned about how he too should have been up for bartender of the year. Rather than stay seated, he stood near our table as he played his verbal violin. Skinny, a dude whose clothes only stayed on him because he tied his belt as tight as possible, Brigham was one of those guys with an A. o. A—an "Absence of Ass." Even belted, the top of his jeans hung closer to the bottom of his butt than the top, showing plenty of waistband and grey boxer-briefs.

As the evening progressed, and one by one our work colleagues went home, I eventually found myself sat alone with Brigham in a booth near the rear of the bar. My introverted self wasn't overly pleased by this, and I found myself wishing Chad would come back to carry the conversation. But my hipster co-worker was too busy chatting up two girls outside in the smoking area.

Brigham offered me a stick of chewing gum and we talked for a while, about nothing in particular—girls, cars, memories from school—the usual things guys like Brigham liked to talk about. But that all changed when he said, "You know Darren Savage, right?"

"Everyone in our neighbourhood knows who Darren is."

"Well, I was hanging out with him yesterday and he was telling me you and his little brother are pretty close."

Like a television chef saying "here's one I prepared earlier", I could tell Brigham had been sitting on this piece of information all night.

"Did he?"

"Like, close, close." His eyes said what his words didn't.

"I-I don't know what you're talking about."

"Don't play stupid, Mike. I ain't gonna tell no one. And even if I did, all you gotta do is deny it. No one's gonna believe me. Shit, even I didn't believe it at first when Darren told me."

Brigham had a point, and it was one that made me drop my guard a bit. "I guess you could say that Jockey and I have an arrangement," I said.

"That's what Darren was saying. An arrangement. Says it's quite a fun one."

"Yeah. It can be fun."

"I never picked you as a queer." He didn't say it rudely, or politely, just more matter of fact. "Had I known that I would have been friendlier at high school."

"Why's that?"

"So you could have sucked my dick," he said with a predatory smile.

I laughed, flustered, unsure of how to respond.

"Okay," I finally said. And then, quieter, almost whispered, almost swallowed: "I would have liked that."

"Is that so?" he asked. His voice had dropped into his throat as he adjusted his package openly, obscenely.

The conversation dried up but an awkward vibe filled with possibilities remained. Had we just flirted? Was that grope he'd just given himself an invite?

I can't say I had ever given Brigham Moss much thought in the sexual sense. He had just been a regular guy I sat next to in Geography, nothing extraordinary about him. But right now I was seized with a desire to know what the skinny rake was packing in his Levis.

I reached over and put my hand on his thigh, lying warm and solid on the denim. He did not move. His face remained immobile as he stared in the direction of the bar. I searched his face for some sign of approval or disapproval, any acknowledgment whatever. None came.

I moved my hand higher until I found the mound of flesh, tight in the crotch of his blue jeans, and I exerted a little pressure. I waited.

Very slowly Brigham spread his legs wider apart, his eyes still looking aimlessly at the bar, and my hand began to massage and rub and squeeze his cock. Across his face there appeared the vestige of a smile, so I relaxed and continued the pressure, more blatantly this time, until I felt his dick stirring and hardening beneath my fingers.

I found the outline of his cock and traced it with my fingers several times, and Brigham moaned lightly. When my hand wandered down to press in on his balls, he squeezed his legs tightly together, trapping my hand between his thighs, and I realised that he must be liking it.

My exploring hand had only been at work a few minutes, however, when Brigham suddenly got up from our booth and made his way outside where Chad was still talking to the two women. The abrupt end to the sexy fumble left me confused. I kept hoping that he would come back, let me touch him some more. But Brigham didn't return to the booth and didn't even look in my direction.

After waiting nearly twenty minutes, and eventually losing sight of him, I finally gave up hope that Brigham would return. I went and said goodbye to Chad and then made my way for the long trek home.

Suddenly, someone called out, "Hey, Mike!"

I looked around. It was Brigham. He was standing in the open doorway of an old Ford parked in one of the white spaces. "Need a ride?" he asked.

I stood there dumbly, an idiot mute.

"Come on, man," he called out. "It's gonna piss down again. You don't wanna be walking in this weather."

I hurried to the car as he got inside behind the wheel. My ready acceptance of a lift had less to do with his dick and more to do with wanting to avoid an hour-long trek home.

Brigham did not ask for directions—he just drove. Maybe he knew where I lived. After all I knew where his parents' home was. When he turned onto the main highway and began to drive out towards the city-limits sign, I wondered what was going on. My hands began to feel damp and I had to clear my voice to speak. "Where are we going?" I asked him.

He glanced at me briefly and a contemptuous smile played on his thin lips for a moment. "I thought you might wanna finish up what you started at the bar," he said.

I did not answer. He flipped on the radio, tuning it in to a rock station.

After about five miles he turned off the main highway into a rest area sheltered by a group of Pohutukawa trees. I tried to keep myself collected, calm, as Brigham turned off the headlights and looked at me, but it was too different, being with somebody out in a car this way. I was embarrassed and a bit frightened and I wished that he had merely taken me home, forgotten all this.

Brigham also was a little uneasy, but he was attempting to disguise it. With an overly casual yawn, he stretched his arms and turned his body beneath the steering wheel so that he was facing me. One knee was elevated, his legs were widespread, and he placed a hand on the crotch of his pants, rubbing his cock through the Levis. His eyes gleamed when they met mine; he was looking up under his brows at me in a funny cocky way that made me suspect

163

he knew things which I did not know and that he had some peculiar advantage over me for the knowledge.

He unbuckled his belt and then slowly undid the buttons on his jeans. I stared, fascinated, unable to look away, unable to speak. I could tell from the growing bulge that he was getting a hard-on and just watching it caused me to have a hard-on also.

He pulled his prick out through the slit of his underwear; it stuck straight out at me through the unbuttoned jeans. It was long and uncut, thin like its owner, with a slight kink that made it point to the right.

Sensing my excitement, Brigham took my hand and placed it around the hard column of flesh, motioning for me to stroke his dick. I did, nervously, fast, jerking him off until he stopped me with his hand and laughed and said, "Not so fast. You'll make me shoot my wad right here."

"Isn't that what you want to do?"

He shrugged one shoulder. "Yeah," he said, "but I'd like to shoot it in something... got me?"

"I get you." My voice was tremulous; I could not take my eyes from his. There was something hypnotic now about his cold, glaring, knowing eyes watching my fear and hesitancy.

His gaze wandered down to my hand on his cock, then back to my eyes. "Shall we go for a walk?" he said.

I nodded and followed his lead by getting out of the car. The walk was all of a few steps to the back of the vehicle. He leaned against the boot, lit a cigarette, and eyed me cautiously.

We didn't speak, just stared at one another. It was drizzling lightly, so lightly that it was more like mist than actual rain. The glowing ember of his cigarette the brightest thing around. He must have only taken three drags on his cigarette before biffing it away and telling me, "You know what to do."

The arrogant command bugged me a little, but he wasn't wrong. I knew what he wanted, and I knew how to do it.

Lowering to my knees, I gave his jeans a savage tug. With nothing to anchor them, no bubble butt to stop the slide, not even the vague appearance of ass cheeks, they and the boxer-briefs beneath flew down Brigham's hairy chicken legs, stopping only at his grubby sneakers.

His sleek cock jutted out at me, and I caught the glistening sweaty flesh between my lips. My tongue instantly registered the bitter tang of piss. He must have wandered off for to the toilets after leaving me in the booth alone. I was too horny to be grossed out.

With an inch of his thin cock in my mouth, I looked up at his face, and he looked down at mine. I didn't see contempt, or even lust. Maybe just an amused curiosity in his slight smile and half-lidded eyes.

"Do you like my dick?" he asked cockily, but I sensed self-doubt beneath the question.

I answered by deepthroating the whole length of him and he let out a long breath that shaded toward a moan. Milking my way back out to the tip, I left his shaft covered in my saliva. I only had to do this a few times before he began to thrust.

I reached up and gripped his lean tight-skinned hips with my hands, digging in with my nails, drawing him furiously to me. After a while, I ran a hand down his leg, over the bony knee, down the hairy calf, to his sneaker-clad foot. Fascinated by how large his feet were in comparison to the rest of him, I used a finger to trace the outline of one his shoes before attempting to undo the laces.

"Leave my feet alone." He shook my hand off his foot. "Just worry about my dick."

Brigham half-closed his eyes and resumed fucking my face. Some unaffected sliver of my consciousness wondered what he imagined through his imagination. Not me, I was sure, as I sucked up and down on his cock. Probably some hot piece of ass, either a former root or a supermodel or some actress from a movie he'd always wanted to bone. While he dreamed, I kept sucking, loving the taste of his sweaty dick.

The musky odour of his maleness possessed me, triggering desires I refused to deny myself. I let his cock slip free then sniffed at his balls, loving their light stink. Then I licked those too, one at a time. The sweat of a long evening coated his nuts. I sucked one, spit it out, and gulped the other before abandoning his balls and returning my attention to his cock.

I took his skinny dick between my lips again, all the way down to his trimmed pubes, loving his boyish taste and odour.

"Oh yeah," he sighed. "Swallow my cock, dude ..."

Dude. Hearing that meant the supermodel or fantasy actress was gone, and he'd returned to seeing me, only me.

I worshipped his cock, with long slow licks, deep swallows and tortuously slow stroking with my lips and tongue. I wanted to give Brigham Moss the best blowjob he'd ever had. Shit, for all I knew maybe this was his first ever blowjob. Whatever the story, I was determined to gift him pleasure and have him feed me the contents brewing in his now tightened balls.

"Bend over the boot," he said suddenly—all breathy, all bossy boy.

Doing as I was told, I released his cock and got to my feet. I turned and grabbed hold of the rear of his vehicle. He reached around and undid the button of my jeans before pulling them down just enough to expose my ass.

The dampness of the air licked my skin and I could feel his eyes burning over my rump. He must have been deciding if he could go through with this or not. It was one thing to let a guy suck you off but to stick your cock up another guy's ass...that was a much bigger decision.

Finally, I heard Brigham spit in his hand and felt his wet finger explore my asshole. The finger slid in wetly. After three careless plunges, it withdrew, and his cock took its place, shoving to get inside my tight little ass. The elastic muscle around the hole tried valiantly to keep him out, but lost the battle. The pain seared to my brain when his shaft finally plunged in.

He was quick, methodical, concerned only with himself and his needs. He ignored my request that he go slowly, be careful, just as he ignored me when I asked him, once he was all the way inside, to wait for a moment in order to allow my asshole time to adjust. He did not speak, perhaps he did not even hear me. He started in right away, stabbing and jabbing and banging me against the back of the car, thrusting his skinny prick in and out of my tortured anus.

I had been reduced to nothing more than a hole, a fuck-hole, something for Brigham Moss to masturbate his cock into. His cock was hard and he wanted to soften it. It was as simple as that.

I don't think even a minute had passed when I felt the hot gushing wetness of his cum spurt deep within my ass, one last thrust, and then it was over. He jerked his prick out of me and took a step back, pulling his jeans back up and putting his dick away.

Sheepishly, sensing that I had been somehow humiliated by his lack of attention and concern for my own excitement, but knowing, definitely knowing that he was finished with me and wanted to go home, I fixed my pants and then got back in the front seat. We drove all the way back to town without speaking, only listening to the radio. I caught a few sideways glances from Brigham. He seemed quite pleased with himself, and satisfied.

When he pulled up in front of my house, he slugged me playfully on the shoulder and said, "Thanks, Mike. I might root you again sometime."

As I walked up the driveway to the front of the house, I pondered his last words. I was both angry and confused as to why he had sounded like he had done me a great favour.

Chapter 17

WHEN I WALKED INSIDE, still able to hear the noisy exhaust of Brigham's car roaring in the distance, I found Gavin and Trent sat at the kitchen table. A half-empty bottle of Coruba rum sat on the centre of the table. Judging by my stepfather's relaxed face muscles he'd drunken most of it.

Trent on the other hand seemed much less inebriated; the sight of me no doubt helping sober him up fast. He fidgeted noticeably in the chair and glanced from side to side as if looking for an emergency exit. Rather than be offended by his apparent wish to escape my presence, I took comfort in the fact I was able to make this burly builder uncomfortable. It was one of the few times I had felt powerful in recent weeks. Maybe that's why instead of taking myself to the toilet and then to bed like I should have, I went and joined them at the table.

"Are you going to join us for a drink?" Gavin asked, his words a lot less slurred than I had expected.

"I think so," I said. "One won't hurt.

Gavin wasted no time in getting up and grabbing me a glass so I could join in with the drinking. Trent's gaze finally met my eyes, just for a second, long enough to shoot me a look that loosely translated to *don't say a fucking word.*

Gavin returned with a glass, filled my drink, then proceeded to update me on the episode of Love Island I'd missed tonight. After giving me a quick rundown, Gavin turned to Trent and asked, "Have you been watching the show?"

Trent shook his head. "I stopped watching the Idiot Box when it lived up to its nickname by making celebrities out of everyday no-talents."

In other words: Love Island. And every other trashy show Gavin and I liked to watch.

"You don't know what you're missing," Gavin said. "Tits and drama. Can't beat it."

"I'll take your word for it," Trent grumbled.

Gavin changed the topic to Betsy and the progress he'd made on her during his week off work. Trent nodded along enthusiastically, looking almost invested as Gavin was about the old hunk of metal that had sat dead in our backyard now for nearly a decade.

Trent laced his hands behind his head. His t-shirt, a yellow number with the phrase *Cheese Slut* across the front, was threadbare and ancient. A rip under one arm showed pale skin and a tangle of armpit hair. Something about his relaxed pose bothered me; like the power of my presence no longer influenced him.

Beneath the table, out of sight, I slipped out of one of my sneakers. The warmth of the evening, coupled by my long walk to the convention centre, had made my size 10s damp with sweat.

Keeping my eyes trained on Trent who was still busy nodding along to Gavin's Betsy story, I stroked my foot down his calf, hooking one long toe beneath the open mouth of his pants leg.

Trent's eyes went wide, and he flinched in his chair.

"You alright?" Gavin asked him. "You look like you seen a ghost?"

"I'm alright," Trent mumbled, flicking me a *fuck-off* glance before looking back to Gavin.

I suppressed a satisfied chuckle and withdrew my foot. Sitting back I picked up my drink, sipping slowly, savouring the burn of the rum.

Trent levelled me with another threatening glare.

Rather than back off, I stroked my foot up his leg again. I smiled when I heard him cough, a distinctive sound of unease. I trailed my foot up his leg, dipping across his thigh until I felt his cock. I curled my toes around the head of his penis, squeezing it until I felt him begin to stiffen.

The cock beneath my foot was loving the attention, but its owner wasn't. Trent squirmed in his seat, even reached under the table twice to try and flick my foot away, but each time I put my foot right back where it had been, massaging his dick to a full erection.

By now Gavin was in the middle of telling us his drunken theory on what was wrong with Wellington bureaucrats when Trent suddenly blurted, "You win."

"I win?" Gavin looked confused. So was I.

"Nothing, mate," Trent said. His eyes narrowed and that Adam's apple flexed as he swallowed a gulp of rum from his glass.

It wasn't until Trent put his drink down and reached under the table that I realised he had been talking to me. Gently nudging my foot out of the way, he discreetly lowered his zipper and fished out his cock, pressing it against the sole of my foot.

After a few strokes, I pulled my foot away to peel the sock off then placed my bare foot on the skin of his burning hot erection.

He visibly shuddered, trying to hide his arousal by an ill-timed chuckle as Gavin spoke. Thankfully my stepfather was too pissed to notice, oblivious to what was going on right under the table.

Soon I had both feet sockless and was jacking Trent's cock between them. I loved how hot the sweaty skin of his cock felt on my soles and toes. Every now and then he'd have to clasp a hand over his mouth to trap a muffled moan, thrusting upward a little as if trying to fuck the tunnel made by my gripping feet.

I was getting turned on by the power running through my veins and just how dangerous this all felt. Social norms would have you believe that a teenage boy shouldn't know the size and taste of their stepfather's best friend's cock, let alone play with it under the table with said stepfather in the same room, but I did and I was, and I gotta say.... I fucking loved it!

Trent was rock-hard and so turned on that I began to feel precum oozing from the tip, dribbling down his shaft onto my toes. He was gagging to fuck his cock to orgasm, but it was just out of reach for him. There just wasn't quite enough friction to give him the homerun he needed, the last bit of *oomph* to trigger that delicious squiggly feeling in his taint and have him fire ropes of come all over my feet.

So close, Trent's eyes were saying. *Just a little harder, Mike. Just a little bit—*

I gave him one more squeeze with my toes, pushing him right to the edge, then pulled my feet away from his sticky cock, depriving the man of the orgasm I'd lured him into wanting. And then I told them both I was going to bed.

"You're what?" Trent uttered, sounding breathless.

"I'm tired," I said. "And I have an early start tomorrow."

"Surely one more drink won't hurt," Trent said, almost begging.

"Yeah, Mikey," Gavin chimed in. "Stay for one more."

I shook my head and got up to leave. I know it was a real dickhead move on my part, but I enjoyed feeling like I was in the driver's seat for a change.

Gavin, completely oblivious to what had been going on, wished me a goodnight's sleep.

Trent sneered in silence.

I swung by the bathroom with the intention of discharging Brigham's semen. I'd been leaking since I'd come home and sat down, and I could feel how stodgy by briefs had become in that short time. I ultimately decided to just take a leak. The feel of Brigham inside me was turning me on too much to be rid of his DNA just yet. I hadn't had a chance to cum when he'd fucked me, so I figured a wank in bed while I fingered myself might be the next best thing.

The stupid thing was that even though I knew Brigham had used me, my anger paled in comparison to regret. I wished I'd have a chance to be with him again so I could properly explore his skinny body, find out just how big those feet of his were. If there was one thing Jockey had imprinted on me it was the desire to know every detail of another man's body.

I'd just finished taking my piss and had gone to wash my hands when Trent walked in the door. We locked eyes in the mirror. He didn't look happy with me.

"What the fuck were you playing at out there?"

"What do you mean?" I said, playing dumb.

"Gavin could have seen what you were doing. Do you think I want my best mate to see his stepson feel my dick up under the table? And then you have the audacity to be a little cocktease! Get me all worked up, gagging for it, and then leave me with blue balls and my dick to the wind."

"I'm sorry, Trent."

"Whatever. Just...don't pull another stunt like that with Gavin around." His eyes lost some of their anger. "And don't start shit you don't intend to finish."

I hesitated. "Did you want me to finish it?"

"No. That's not why I came in here. I just wanted you to know not to pull another stupid stunt like that again. Got me?"

I nodded. "Sorry again. I don't know what I was thinking."

"You weren't thinking." He finally cracked a smile. "Not with your big brain at least."

I thought that was it and I turned to finish washing my hands but I froze as Trent reached out and placed a hand firmly on the small of my back, right at the top of my butt cheeks. "You're just lucky I can't stop thinking about this sweet ass of yours," he said as he began to lightly run his hand up and down my butt cheeks. "Otherwise I would have been really mad."

I stood there motionless, completely caught off guard and unsure how to respond as he stood next to me, rubbing my ass.

His hands suddenly reached around and unbuttoned the front of my jeans. "Don't worry," he whispered, holding my gaze in the mirror. "I only wanna look." He then dragged my pants down, past my knees, and stepped back to admire my ass.

"Yep." He whistled low and slow. "That's one fine ass you have there, young Michael. One very fine ass indeed."

"Thanks," I replied timidly.

"That ass of yours milked more loads out of me in one night than Donna has in two years."

"Really?"

He nodded, still staring. "The frigid bitch has only spread her legs once since the twins were born. Can you believe it? Once in two years."

"That's...that's a long time."

Even though I could feel my dick getting hard, I didn't dare touch it. Something about playing with yourself while a married man rubs your ass and complains about his wife just feels wrong.

Smiling, Trent said, "Had I known how easy it was to get it up for a bloke I might have tried it years ago. I certainly enjoyed it more than I thought I would." He laughed softly. "Maybe mine and Gavin's deal about getting married at thirty if we were both single wasn't such a stupid idea."

"Maybe not," I whispered, wondering when he would say I could pull my pants up.

Trent put his hand on my bare ass, rubbing slowly up and down, and he slipped his middle finger in the cleft between my cheeks. I gasped when he suddenly pressed deeper into my ass crack, finding my slick, slack hole with his middle finger. The tip of his finger swirled gently around my hole, nudging ever so slightly into my recently-fucked anus.

I watched his reflection in the mirror above the sink. He was grinning, a horny grin, pushing his finger a little deeper. When he retrieved his digit he glanced down, frowning. Pretty soon that frown had turned into a grimace and he locked eyes with me in the mirror. "Is that cum on my finger?"

He sounded like a father asking if I'd stolen money from his wallet. My tummy twisted, unsure what to say.

"Um..."

"It is, isn't it?"

A denial swelled in my throat, but he knew. There were zero doubts in those hazel eyes of his.

Trent sighed, washing a cool breath across the back of my neck, and the scintillating shudder cascaded down my back to my ass; and to my front, engulfing my cock in ripples of pleasure.

The disgust slowly faded from his face but it remained in his voice. "You been out slutting, have ya? Letting all the boys cornhole your backdoor?"

"Just one boy."

"Yeah, like I said... *slutting*."

He said that last word with pure hatred and jabbed his soiled finger back inside my asshole. I stood frozen in place as Trent took a step closer to me, letting his middle finger slide much deeper into my slick opening, squishing around the cum that Brigham had pumped into me less than an hour ago. I gasped involuntarily as I felt his thick finger sinking deeper into my opening but I made no move to stop him, and in fact I had instinctively started to push back against his finger.

Trent began to swirl that middle finger in a circular motion, working it all around inside me. The noises were obscene; a wet squelching that left no doubt as to the amount of semen Brigham had filled me with.

"So who fucked this ass of yours?" he asked "Was it your master?"

Body squirming, I responded to his question, "No. Someone else. A friend."

"Does this friend have a name?"

I shuddered and sighed when he plunged in a second finger. "B-Brigham."

Trent's eyes were focused on his fingers sliding in and out of my passage. "Well, you can tell Brigham from me that his balls shoot big loads. You're fucking filled with the stuff. Dirty slut."

I couldn't be sure if this was dirty talk or hate talk, either way he was fingering me to an erection.

"Do you like them boys spunking inside ya do you, Mike? You like having a juicy faggot hole?"

I bit my lip to stifle a whimper of pleasure and excitement. "Yeah..." I sighed.

"You oughta let a real man fuck you then...really give you what you need."

Hearing him say these words brought instant clarity to this surreal situation: we were going to fuck. And it was gonna happen right here in the bathroom while Gavin sat half-sloshed down the hall. I contracted my ass muscles to give his fingers a little squeeze. "Yes. I'd like that, sir."

I leaned over the sink, smudging my hands against the mirror, eagerly presenting my ass to my stepfather's best mate as he unzipped behind me. Trent then held me firmly by the hips as he bumped his fat cock head against my anus. "You ready for this dick?" he asked.

Without a word I pushed myself back against his cock, causing the head to pop inside me. The abrupt entry caused me to give out a yelp of surprise. "Ooh!" I cried, my voice going a little higher than usual.

"Shhh." His breath against my skin raised the fine hairs on the back of my neck.

I turned my face to the right and buried my open mouth on my own biceps. It was the only way I could think of to muffle my response as he buried himself deeper.

I thought taking Trent's thick cock might be painful, but the load Brigham had left in me was making everything nice and slick, and he was able to sink over halfway in without causing me any pain at all. I pushed back, hard, forcing more of his cock to enter my body.

I moaned. I might have said some words but they came out as unintelligible little yelps. Trent's cock was buried all the way inside me. I could feel it twitching.

Feeling his shaft pull through the ring of my asshole and shove itself back through was a dizzying delight. I arched my back more, lifting my ass higher. I certainly enjoyed his dick more than Brigham's. For one thing, Trent was thicker and able to stretch me the way I knew Jockey could, but the older man was also more experienced than Brigham and it showed. It didn't matter that his experience had come from fucking women, Trent just seemed more aware how to make me moan and shiver.

Each time I felt Trent's cock slide into me, I'd squeeze him with my asshole causing my own cock to nod and stiffen. Occasionally I would push back to meet his thrust, plunging his cock deeper inside my body.

"You want it don't cha?" he gritted out. "You want all this daddy juice."

"Mmhmm," I moaned. "Gimme the lot."

I was too far gone to care what he called his cum. He could call it what he liked, as long as he gave me every drop.

With my head tilted upwards, my eyes soared across the ceiling, seeing nothing. I was busy taking in the sensation of being spread open by cock. Trent's calloused hands explored my legs and my ass. He gave it to me at an enjoyable pace—not too rough, not too soft, just right.

Then I was grabbed tightly by both hips. Trent shifted behind me and began to fire his hips into me. The sudden change of gears caught me off balance. Now my ass was being assaulted. Trent's hips slammed into me with such force that my legs hit the sink cabinet violently. It hurt. It was incredible. I felt powerless.

I was locked in Trent's grasp. I'd never truly been at the mercy of anything like this before. Not even Jockey had dished it out so severely. I was just being held and fucked. Everything that happened now was willed by Trent. I grasped the edge of the basin to keep my balance, the surface slippery beneath my fingers. I let Trent pound himself through me because I couldn't do anything else.

Trent then pressed himself against me as tightly as he could, wrapping an arm around my chest. He held still, panting in my ear, and after a few moments I felt his dick began to spurt, filling me with seed. I'd never felt anything like it, such a slow and forceful cum. Each time his dick twitched he would sigh a little more. It went on and on, so long that I swore it must have set a world record for the longest ejaculation.

By the time he'd finished spunking, still breathing hard in my ear, my anus was filled to the brim with the man's warmth. Even with his dick still inside me I could feel some of the hot sperm escaping, running down my crack, bathing my balls, dripping down the backs of my legs.

"My ass has never felt so full," I whispered. "You must have really needed to cum."

"I didn't cum," he said.

"Huh?"

He eased his cock out and I felt more wetness escape. "I didn't cum," he said again.

"But—" I reached around to touch my asshole and felt an alarming amount of fluid trickling out.

"I don't cum inside sluts. They're not worthy of my *daddy juice*." His voice got even nastier. "But I will piss in them."

I watched my own reaction in the mirror, the slow and disturbing realisation of what he'd just done. How the hell had I been so stupid? No man could shoot that much jizz *and* for that long.

"You fucking wanker," I whisper-shouted.

Trent chuckled to himself and wiped his dick clean on my ass.

As much as I wanted to punch him right now, I didn't dare spin around; worried than any sudden movement would see me eject the contents inside my ass all over the carpet. "Why the hell would you piss in me?"

"Don't get snarly with me, Nancy. You're the one who told me you like having a juicy hole. And like I said...I don't cum in sluts."

I was livid. And humiliated. And—

Still horny as fuck.

Trent gave my ass a playful pat and winked at me in the mirror. "Cheers for letting me use the pisser."

And without another word, he left me there in the bathroom with an ass full of piss and the knowledge of just how tainted I had become.

Chapter 18

GAVIN WAS DOODLING on a notepad at the dining table. I sat across from him, enjoying his scent, watching his lips, listening to him tell me his plans for the day, telling him mine. He sipped the coffee I'd just made him, commenting on how good it was, while my eyes trailed over the dark stubble that rode his upper lip, masqueraded as sideburns, and peppered his chin.

The handsome sight was the pickup I needed after last night's twisted events. Not just once, but twice in the same evening, I had allowed a man to use me for their own enjoyment. Brigham's selfish venture had probably just been a case of horny curiosity, using me as a convenient place to put his cock and make himself feel like a man in the process. And as for Trent? The animal had used me to...to what? I wasn't even sure I knew the right words for that.

It was only ten o'clock but Gavin had already mowed the lawns and had plans to spend the afternoon working on Betsy. His sprightliness amazed me after how much he'd drunk last night, but he didn't appear the least bit hungover. I suppose it helped that he'd been drinking rum—his preferred poison.

I watched Gavin's drawing hand, admiring his long fingers, imagining what it would feel like to have him place them on my body. I may have only been 24 hours away from officially becoming another man's property, but right now all I craved was one look, one touch, one taste, of what my stepfather had to offer.

I tried to reason why I was suddenly noticing Gavin in a sexual way. Until this week I hadn't had an improper thought about him since I was fifteen. I mean sure, I had still considered him handsome—for an older dude—but I'd stopped fantasising about him a long time ago. It unnerved me a bit because nothing had really changed in our relationship to reignite this crush. It wasn't as if anything about him had changed. He was still the same belching, farting, beer-drinking blue-collar bloke he'd always been. And yet, more and more, I was finding myself thinking about what he'd look like naked—naked and standing over me.

Maybe I should have let Stryder fuck him, I thought. At least that way I could have asked the blond teen what Gavin looked like naked. Now all I had to go on was the occasional glimpses I'd stolen of him through the years walking about the house in his underwear.

"I can't wait to get back to work tomorrow," Gavin said, eyes focused on the picture he was doodling. "It's been dead boring stuck at home this week."

"Maybe you should have gone away and done something," I suggested. "At least that way you wouldn't have been stuck at home as much."

"I don't know how you do it."

"Do what?"

"Not work fulltime."

"I practically do work fulltime," I said, mildly offended. "I've already worked twenty hours this week. And after today's shift that'll make it twenty-eight."

Gavin sniggered under his breath. "That's nothing."

"And when I'm not at the café then I'm busy working on my novel."

"That's a hobby, Mike. It doesn't count."

"It won't be a hobby if I can get an agent."

Rather than dismiss that pipedream, Gavin nodded in agreements. "It's criminal that you haven't been signed by one yet. You're a talented little bugger and deserve to be published."

"Thanks, but to be fair you've never read anything I've written. They very well could be a steaming pile of shit."

He stopped doodling for a moment and looked over at me. "I'd love to read one of your stories but you won't let me."

"Yeah, cause I'm worried their shit."

"They won't be shit. You've talked to me enough about them through the years for me to know you at least have an idea of what makes a good story. That would be half the battle, I reckon."

Gavin's belief in me was nice, but I was also aware this was a man whose reading habits didn't extend much past the sport pages in the newspaper.

My stepfather returned to the picture he was doodling. One of his hands was in the way so I couldn't see what it was. He was actually a pretty good drawer—and made an excellent partner when playing Pictionary—but most of the pages in his notepad were filled with murals of random squares and circles—artistic in a basic bitch sort of way.

"Had I known Fiona was going away with the kids for the weekend I would never have taken the week off. There's nothing to fucking do cause I feel like I've already reached my Netflix and chill quota for the week."

"There's always the dishes," I said cheekily.

Gavin cast a wincing glance in the direction of the kitchen bench. It was still a cluttered mess, and once again the faint odour of rotting food was permeating the place. I had very nearly washed them up last night but Gavin had told me not to, insisting it was his turn and that he would wash them before bed. He hadn't, of course.

"Fucking dishes," he muttered.

"Maybe it's time we get a dishwasher," I suggested.

"But then you gotta stack the fucking thing and empty it." He sighed. "I'm waiting for the day they build a robot maid like they have in the Jetsons."

"Dreams are free, I guess."

Dropping the pen in his hand, Gavin pushed his chair back, giving me the perfect view of his crotch and pants-clad legs. It was a sexier sight than it ought to be on account of a hole as big as my palm in the upper thigh of his sweatpants.

I glanced down at Gavin's bare leg shining out through the hole. At his muscular leg with the sprinkling of coarse, dark hair. I wanted to get up, walk around the table, and set my hand on that bare leg. Feel the heat and strength surging through his flesh into my own. I wanted to massage that thigh, feel it lift and move off to the side, giving me access to the heavy basket it walled. I could see Gavin's underwear though the hole; a pair of red briefs that were so old they'd almost faded to pink.

I took a sip on my coffee and watched as he scratched his leg though the hole in the sweatpants. His fingers running just under the underwear. When he pulled his fingers out a thick tuft of pubic hair stuck out under the leg band, curling around it like a beckoning finger. Seeming to say to me, *What you want is in here. Come and get it.* I looked at it and felt a familiar ache growing in me again.

I imagined myself moving in between Gavin's legs, pushing his thighs apart while my mouth worked at that hole in his pants, widening it, tearing strips of the material free. In my fantasy I was like a hungry dog, snuffling at Gavin's body, snorting and lapping my way into his crotch. I could taste the salty tang of the thin layer of sweat coating Gavin's thighs and when I worked my way into the crease of my stepfather's leg, had the first glimmer of the heat and raw power of what awaited me beneath the underwear.

"Are you meeting up with your sexy vampire tonight?"

Snapping myself out of my reverie, I exhaled; unaware I'd been holding my breath so tight. "What's that?"

"Are you meeting up with your sexy vampire tonight?"

"I'm not sure yet. I'm working the late shift today so probably not."

"Seriously, Mikey, it's time you introduce us. I'm dying to see who this fella is."

"Soon," I said. "You'll meet him soon."

"I hope so. With your mother not around it's up to me to make sure you're making good choices." He sounded like a real parent there for a moment. But that illusion was shattered with his next breath. "I won't have you sticking your dick in any uglies. You'll bring our household into disrepute."

I laughed, hoping Gavin wouldn't press for any more details.

I should have told him by now who the sexy vampire was. Jockey clearly didn't give a shit if Gavin knew about us. But I did for some reason. Maybe because I was worried that Jockey would not hesitate in telling my stepfather the true nature of our relationship—owner and faggot. Aside from the fact it would be embarrassing, I knew Gavin would have something to say about it.

185

"Well, I suppose I better go to town and buy these parts for Betsy." He got up from his chair and went and placed his coffee mug amongst the Mt Everest of dirty dishes on the bench. "When I get back I'll make a start on these fucking dishes."

"I can do the dishes before I go to work if you want."

"You don't have to do that. It's my turn. Has been for days."

"It's no big deal. I don't have to be at work until twelve."

He reached down, dug his finger into the hole of his pants again, and scratched under his balls. "Are you sure?"

I nodded, my mouth dry, trying not to stare at him stirring his balls around.

"You're a scholar and a gentleman, Michael Freeman. I'll owe you one."

Without thinking, dangerous words leapt from my tongue. "You can pay me with a pair of your undies."

Gavin's eyebrows climbed in surprise. "My what? My undies?"

Instead of laughing the comment away like a bad joke, my dickmatized state forced me to follow through. "You said the other day that if I did the dishes for you then you'd give me a pair of your dirty underwear."

A slow smile spread across his lips. "Be careful what you wish for, Mikey, I might just come good on that request."

"That's what I want," I said honestly.

Gavin laughed. "It would take a brave man to want what the pair I'm wearing. I've had them on for three days now."

"Even better."

He eyed me warily, like he was finally realising how serious I was.

I bit down on a tender part of my lip, almost too hard.

Gavin's focus zoomed in, pupils dilating. His dark lashes lowered like shields over his emotions, and he raked a hand through his hair.

His sudden silence made a ruthless meal out of my nerves until the hairs on my nape jumped away from my skin. My heart was thundering. We were on the edge of a cliff we could never return. I should have been back peddling, telling him it was a joke, but my arousal wouldn't let me.

Gavin's suspicion abruptly ended when he began to laugh again. "You crack me up, matey. You really had me going there for a moment."

And on that note, he walked off leaving me alone with a pile of dishes to wash without reward.

Chapter 19

ASIDE FROM BEING ANNOYED at lumbering myself with a pile of filthy dishes that took me so long to wash I was ten minutes late for work, I had decided it was a blessing Gavin had thought I was joking. Like, how fucked up would life at home be if he'd known I was serious? Shit would have got majorly awkward, the pair of us probably unable to be in the same room together, and I'm sure it would only have sped up my inevitable eviction.

Fiona may not have been in any hurry to get married, and neither was Gavin now that he'd come to his senses, but that didn't mean they wouldn't end up moving in together. If my memory was correct then Jockey and Fiona had been discussing living together after only dating for about three months. The only thing that had stopped it from happening was Fiona's mother had moved in with her while looking for a new apartment, and she didn't move out of Fiona's house until Jockey and Fiona had split up. Well, Fiona's mother had her own place now which meant nothing would stop Gavin and Fiona having the 'let's live together' talk.

All the more reason to embrace being Jockey's bitch.

I had already decided that once I became accustomed to Jockey's kinky demands, which I'm sure would take some getting used to, then I would ask him about us living together. I would get some much-needed security and my perpetually horny master would get easier access to my body. It seemed like a win-win.

What wasn't a win-win was working tonight's shift with my boss Carol. She rarely came to work at all these days, just paid a senior member of her staff to manage the café/bar for her, and if she did come in then she never ever stayed on past four o'clock. But she had no choice tonight after she'd agreed to give Chad the night off. I suppose she thought she'd find it easy to find someone willing to cover her son's shift—she had thought wrong.

Now I was forced to spend the last half of my eight-hour shift working under Carol's watchful eye. And boy was it watchful. The woman could spot a beer spill a mile away, and her voice was loud enough to be heard from that distance barking out the order to wipe it up. To be fair, she was usually a very nice lady, warm and quite motherly to her staff, but clearly she had no desire to act as a barmaid in her own establishment. That required effort. And she preferred to pay people to effort for her.

When Carol had made me re-mop the kitchen floor after telling me "The floor is still filthy, Mike. I'm not paying you to be lazy, now do it again!" I had very nearly told her to go fuck herself. That was normally how I handled bossy bitches, bark back without thinking. Unfortunately this approach to life's more patience-thinning interactions had cost me my last two jobs. I knew I couldn't do that again. Not just because I needed the money but because I sensed it would make Jockey mad. The army-obsessed stoner was all about hard work, loyalty and respecting authority—and that included managers.

Maybe that was a good thing to come out of signing that contract. Some of my master's good points were wearing off on me and I was learning to respect authority. Or at least pretend to.

Crouched behind the bar, I was now busy restocking one of the fridges when I heard Carol call my name again. "Mike?"

I slowly rose up and turned to see Carol standing in the doorway of the kitchen. "I'm just going out back to the office for my break. Call me if you need me."

I nodded before glancing around at our zero customers. I wouldn't be needing her.

With Carol gone, I felt safe to take my phone out and turn it on. Right away it bleeped with a series of unseen messages.

Gavin: Donna and the kids are still away so Trent's asked if we want to come play some pool at his house 2nite? Let me know if you do. Trent said he doesn't mind paying for an uber to pick you up from work.

The next two messages were from a number I didn't recognise but the texter's identity wasn't hard to work out.

Unknown: Did Gav tell u to come over 2nite? I'll pay for the uber. I was thinking we could play a game where I see how many times I can fuck you without Gavin realising what we're doing ;) Sound fun? Otherwise I'll just have to have a wank LOL

Unknown: And sorry about the other night. I was really drunk. But you gotta admit that was pretty hot rite? Hoping u mite let me piss in u again.

Unknown: I dnt mind u keeping my number but try not 2 txt anything 2 faggy. I dnt want the wife or Gavin seeing those sorts of messages.

I rolled my eyes. Clearly someone's balls were getting the better of him. What was Trent's plan? Get Gavin so drunk he passed out? Sneak me into the bathroom every time he felt horny and fuck me over a handbasin again? As resentful as I still was at the man who had turned me into a human urinal my dick wasn't holding a grudge, and I felt myself get hard at the thought of the hairy builder fucking me all over his house. Hell, I'd probably let him piss in me again if he fucked me good enough.

Before responding and committing to a night of being sneakily buggered behind Gavin's back, I checked the fourth and final message.

Jockey: Cum 2 my place after work. I want u here to witness Damian signing the contract. I've told him 2 be here by 11.

It turned out the choice to visit Trent's was made for me—I wouldn't be going. My master's wishes trumped Trent's any day of the week. And with any luck Damian wouldn't turn up to sign the contract, leaving a dissatisfied Jockey with an angry boner he'd need a hole to unleash his frustration on.

With great satisfaction, I replied to Trent's messages: *Maybe another time. Have a nice wank.*

Chapter 20

"IT'S NEARLY MIDNIGHT!"

Jockey's usually relaxed voice was strained. He was pacing back and forward, constantly glancing at the time on his phone. Outside the moon was bright and full, stars galore in the sky, and an unseasonal chill in the air. But inside Jockey's sleepout the air was heated by his brewing anger and thinning patience.

"That thieving prick was supposed to be here an hour ago." Jockey came to an abrupt stop in the middle of the room. "Where the fuck is he?"

I could have told him Damian wouldn't turn up, but I hadn't wanted to ruin his good mood. He'd been all smiles when I first arrived two hours ago, telling me how excited he was to own two faggots. Rather than take offense at his eagerness to bring another guy into the mix, I'd just sat on the sleepout floor, nodding and smiling to Jockey's kinky plans.

But those smiles and that eager tone were long gone now.

"You'd think he would at least have the decency to text me and say he's running late."

I nodded again.

"It's so fucking rude. You don't make the man who's about to own your ass wait." Jockey exhaled and ran a hand over his head. "If he pulls this shit after he's signed the contract then he'll be taught a lesson. Bastard."

While Jockey continued to pace and moan, I picked up the copy of Damian's contract I'd been allowed to read while we waited for my former babysitter to arrive. According to Jockey it was important that Damian and I were aware of each other's responsibilities.

For the most part the contract was pretty similar to the one I had signed, but there were a few differences. The main one being that Jockey expected half of whatever money Damian made through whoring at Hickford Park. There was even a clause dictating what evenings Jockey would allow my former babysitter to go there. Another difference was there was no delayed start date. The moment Damian handed back the signed contract Jockey would have full ownership of his ass. I sort of envied that. I didn't like this limbo state I was in; sort of owned, sort of not owned.

"I'm starting to think he isn't coming," Jockey said.

Well, duh! I could have told you that.

If anyone knew how crazy someone had to be to sign away ownership of their body then it would be me. And my situation had been totally different to the one Damian was facing. My reasons for signing the contract had been emotional; specifically my fear of abandonment. That wasn't an issue for Damian, and I wasn't convinced the prospect of prison time would force his hand either. He'd gone away before so it wasn't like he wasn't used to life behind bars. Jockey though did point out that the longest Damian had been inside was six months—a far cry from the four to five years he could face for yet another charge.

As I read the last page of Damian's contract, I found something else not included in mine:

If you decide to become my faggot then you will be expected to attend pussy training school for the first week. I will cover any expenses associated with your stay there. But do remember: A faggot's behaviour is a reflection on their alpha so I expect you to show your host the upmost respect.

"Jockey?"

"Yeah?"

"What's..." I glanced at the contract again before uttering the ridiculous phrase, "pussy training school?"

Jockey surveyed me for a moment and then flashed me one of his wicked grins. "It's not an actual school or anything. Just some guy who said he'd look after Damian for a few days so you and me can spend some quality time together. That way I can be sure Damian's pussy is getting fed regularly while I concentrate on fucking the shit out of yours. You're my number one bitch. He's number two."

I figured there was a compliment aimed at me in there somewhere; buried beneath the twisted way Damian was being treated like a dog being sent to stay at a pet hotel.

"So who's the guy Damian has to stay with?" I asked.

"It's a mate of Darren's. He lined it up for me."

"So Darren knows about Damian too?"

"Of course. We're brothers. We tell each other everything."

Maybe it was because I was an only child but I found Jockey's need to tell his brother absolutely every detail about his life a bit fucking weird. Surely it paid to keep some secrets to yourself. Didn't it?

"Does Darren know many gay guys?" It was a loaded question. And Jockey picked up on it.

"Darren's not gay," he said defensively. "And neither is this guy. He's an alpha male. There's a difference."

"So is Darren is into this hierarchy thing too?"

"Not really. He just knows lots of people. Dealers. Gangstas. Kinksters. You know how popular he is. Darren's the coolest."

Jockey's adoration of Darren was strangely sweet, but also infuriating. How could he not see through Darren's try-hard tough guy act? Beneath the sneers, mangy tattoos, and criminal record, was just a wannabe gangsta about as hard as cotton candy.

Five minutes later, Jockey's pacing came to a stop right in front of me.

"It doesn't look like Damian is showing up," he finally conceded. "I don't suppose you would mind sucking my dick to cheer me up?"

"I don't mind." The words left my mouth faster than lightening. "You can fuck me too if you want?"

Jockey laughed, but did not comment.

My hand reached for his fly, eager—no, desperate—to free the beautiful cock in those army pants. I pinched the hot brass of the zipper and pulled it down, releasing the musky heat trapped inside his pants. I reached into the dark crevasse of his fly. He wasn't wearing underwear. My fingers met a moist tangle of hair, and then the warm, soft flesh of his cock. But before I could pull it out, a light knock sounded at the door.

Flicking my hand away, Jockey zipped his pants up and stormed past me to open the door.

It was Damian. And he was holding a white envelope.

"Your late," Jockey said sternly.

Responding with a grunt, Damian stepped inside, more casual than I had anticipated—until he saw me sat on the floor.

"What the fuck is he doing here?" Damian growled. "I thought it was just gonna be you and me?"

"Mike is here because I invited him."

Damian's expression flickered. "I was rather hoping we could talk about this in private."

"Well, what you want and what you get are two different things," Jockey said. "So are you going to sign the contract or what?"

Damian hesitated. "That's what I wanted to talk with you about. I thought we could come to a different sort of agreement."

"Such as?"

"Such as maybe I swing by once or twice a week and let you get your jollies with me. We don't need to have something as official as this." Damian raised the envelope he was holding and gave Jockey a smile. "You're not a bad-looking guy. I don't mind if you want to bum me now and then. For free."

"Now and then?"

"Like once or twice a week."

Jockey laughed. "I don't think so."

"Three times a week?" Desperation painted Damian's face. "Four? Four times a week."

"I'm gonna stop you right there," Jockey said. "The contract isn't up for debate. You either become my full-time faggot or you can go back to prison where I'm sure you'll be someone else's."

They stared each other down for a moment, like two cats fighting over territory. I was waiting for Damian to lose his shit, throw a punch maybe, but he remained calm. Disturbingly so.

Then, nodding more to himself than to Jockey, Damian finally said, "You better go get me a pen then so I can sign the dotted line."

That's it? You're not going to fight or argue? You're just gonna sign it?

I knew I was supposed to be quiet, like a child seen and not heard, but I couldn't not say anything. "But, Damien, have you even read the contract? You don't want to put your name to something you don't understand."

This earned me disapproving sneers from both men.

"I'm not a fucking idiot, Mike," Damian hissed. "Of course I've read the contract. More than once. And I understand it."

I frowned. "And you're fine with it?"

"I guess I have to be. It's either that or four to five years in jail." Damian let out a friendly snicker as fake as Jockey's army credentials. "Besides, it's not the end of the world. And it's only for a year, right?"

Jockey nodded. "That's right."

"To be honest," Damian replied, "I was actually impressed with how fair the contract is. I hadn't expected that. You sound like a man who knows what he's doing and I respect that. I like that."

"Uh, thanks," Jockey said, looking every bit as surprised as I was at seeing how cool Damian seemed with everything.

After Jockey grabbed from me his own copy of Damian's contract, the pair went and sat down at the small table near the kitchenette where Jockey went over the contract with his newest recruit, page by page, explaining very clearly what was expected of both of them. For the most part Damian just nodded along, listening, rarely saying anything other than "Yeah" or "Okay". It wasn't until Jockey got to the section about the tattoo that Damian said anything more. Unlike my contract that had given me the option between getting a tattoo or a video of me being fucked at Hickford Park, Damian's contract only gave him the tattoo option.

Which I suppose didn't really make it an option so much as an order.

"What will the tattoo say exactly?" Damian asked.

"I will give you a few options to choose from but each one will contain my name. I like to name my property."

"And it'll be in a place no one can see it, right?"

"Only those who fuck you might see it."

Damian looked reluctant but still nodded. "Okay."

As I sat on the floor and watched, I could not help but acknowledge how much Jockey was in his element. In his own unique way he was good at this sort of thing. He could make the absurd sound reasonable, and he was able to word it in a way that was almost comforting. There were even a couple moments where Damian enthusiastically agreed with what was being offered; like the part where Jockey talked about the possibility of moving out of his sleepout and renting a house closer to town.

"If I rent my own place then I would make sure it has a room you can have of your own," Jockey said. "No more staying in a caravan. No more worrying about ending up homeless. You'd have a permanent home with everything you need, including decent meals and a hot shower."

"That would be pretty awesome," Damian agreed.

"Just think how nice and clean your balls will be for the johns at Hickford Park."

Damian sniggered. "That's true."

"Which brings me to the income clause..." Jockey pointed his pen at the page. "I expect fifty per cent of whatever you earn at Hickford Park. I don't care if it's twenty dollars or two thousand dollars. Half of what you earn comes to me. It's not going to be cheap caring and providing for two faggots so I need you to do your part."

I expected some push back to this but to my astonishment all Damian said was, "Fair enough, bro."

I wondered if he would be as easy-going about it if he knew I wasn't expected to split what I earned from my job. Probably not.

The next part of the contract saw Damian fill out the sections asking him for his measurements and to share intimate details of his sexual history. This was done in silence—Damian writing and Jockey reading his answers—so I wasn't able to learn any of my former babysitter's secrets. The only part I was privy to was the man's masturbation habits when Jockey blurted: "You only wank once a week? Bullshit."

While I shared in Jockey's disbelief I did also wonder if that said more about us than it did about Damien.

"It's the truth," said Damian. "If I'm gonna nut then I prefer to do it while I'm fucking."

"You score often enough not to have to wank every day?" Jockey raised an incredulous brow. "With women?"

"I've always done more than alright with the ladies," Damian said with a seedy smile. "Plus it pays not to unload the gun too much if I'm going to the park to try and make some cash."

"That makes sense," Jockey said.

It still baffled me how Damian Takarangi had maintained such a steady supply of women since losing his gym muscles and becoming so drug-fucked. But I guess the sexual company he kept didn't have high standards. To be fair though, he wasn't ugly or anything, and he did have that confidence women seemed to like in a guy—even if it was drug induced these days.

Eventually they came to the last page of the contract where all that was left to do was for Damian to sign his name. Clenched between long, trembling fingers, the pen shook as Damian hesitated. He started laughing quietly.

"What's so funny?" Jockey asked.

Damian shook his head. "Nothing. I just can't believe I'm about to sign something like this. You really stitched me up, didn't you?"

This was the first proper mention of how Jockey had set Damian up, and it certainly soured the vibe in the room.

"I'm not forcing you to do anything," Jockey said. "It's your choice if you sign it or not."

"It's not really my choice though, is it?"

Another staring contest ensued, only broken when Jockey replied, "We always have a choice."

With a heavy sigh, Damian put pen to paper and signed his name. "There you go, boss. My ass is officially yours."

The look of hunger in Jockey's eyes was downright carnivorous. He eyed my former babysitter head to toe, like he couldn't wait to dine on his flesh. It was perhaps only then that I appreciated how patient Jockey was. He didn't rush things; sex or vengeance. Rather he liked to wait and savour his victories.

"What happens now?" Damian asked.

"Now you take your clothes off so we can do your inspection. I need to make sure your measurements match what you have written in the contract. And then... I'm going to fuck you." Jockey spoke with about as much warmth as a prostate exam. "I firmly believe a faggot needs his master's cum in his ass to really seal the deal."

"I s'pose it's a good thing I took a shit before coming here then."

If Damian thought such a vulgar comment would somehow dampen Jockey's desire, he was wrong. Jockey didn't look the least bit thrown off his game. The scruffy stoner simply pointed to the centre of the room and told Damian to stand in that spot and undress.

When Damian got down to just his underwear—a surprisingly nice and clean pair of black jockey shorts, which I assumed he had put on for the occasion—Jockey told him to lay down on the floor.

Damian looked confused. "You don't want me to take my undies off too?"

"Not yet. Just lay down."

"Okay, boss."

Expressionless, yet with a tacit air of arrogance about him that absorbed and aroused me, Jockey stared down at Damian lying half-naked on the floor. Their eyes were locked, silent words exchanged, and a crisp awareness settled over the room. What struck me most about what I was seeing was how both men seemed intrinsically aware of their role. It occurred to me that perhaps Damian had dealt with similar scenarios before, evenings where men would pay him to play pretend, but this time the power game was permanent.

"Come sit over here, Mike," Jockey said. "I want you to come and get a good look at your fag brother."

Shuffling over, I sat on my knees near Damian's right hip. I could tell my closer presence was making Damian uncomfortable, I didn't blame him, but he was doing an admirable job of acting natural.

Jockey hunched down beside me, his voice rolling seductively into my ear: "Over the next twelve months you will get to know Damian's body as good as your own, and mine. You're going to know what every inch of his skin tastes like. Where his tickle spots are. And how best to get him off. You will become so aware of his body's wants and needs that he won't even have to tell you what they are or when he needs them met." Jockey then directed his sexy voice at Damian. "Same goes for you. You're going to learn every inch of Mike's body. Sweat, blood, piss and shit, you'll taste it all."

Damian glanced up at me and we shared a look of *oh fuck*.

"You're both beautiful boys in your own way," Jockey said like a proud parent. "And I am proud to own both of you. Like all siblings you two are bound to argue sometimes but I will be on hand to sort out any squabbling. I also promise to treat you both equally. There may be times where one of you feels neglected but that doesn't mean I don't care. It just means I'm more in the mood to fuck your brother's pussy. That's all."

A rolling shiver passed through Damian's body, probably a ripple of disgust similar to the one rolling through my stomach. This daddy-like role Jockey was suddenly playing felt strange, icky, like he was putting an outfit on that didn't fit. It was easy to view him as a young, dark master... but a father figure? That was a stretch.

"Touch your brother," Jockey said to me. "Explore him. Learn him. Love him."

Starting at Damian's shoulder, I let my fingers stray down over his pectorals and across his belly. I proceeded to play with the silky strands of hair encircling the belly button, excited by the way the hairs blossomed into greater fullness as they disappeared beneath the band of the jockey shorts.

My hand leapt over his crotch, too embarrassed to touch him there yet, and went to his thighs. I could feel the heat coming from his balls as I stroked the soft flesh of his inner thighs. I might have been following Jockey's orders right now but that didn't mean I wasn't enjoying what I was doing. I thought to myself how I would have liked to have done something similar the night I had paid Damian for sex; take my time, familiarise myself with his body. Unfortunately that night hadn't gone to plan, and this felt like a second chance.

Becoming more brazen, I let my hand glide over Damian's cotton briefs. I rubbed the material which was moulded around his genitals. While we were similar sizes when erect, we were very different when flaccid—which Damian currently was. My dick when soft was paltry and boyish but his was respectable and manly.

"How does he feel?" Jockey asked. "And be honest."

"Nice...warm...sexy," I replied, whispering in what was a tone of guilt. "I like touching him here."

"If you like touching your brother there that much why don't you give it a kiss?"

I gave a nod before leaning my face into Damian's crotch. Right away I could tell that beneath the material things were less clean, and it was safe to say he hadn't had a shower for a few days. But the smell was all male, virile, and I gladly inhaled the funk of his balls. I rubbed my cheek along the ridge of the concealed cockshaft, feeling him grow beneath me. He let out a sharp breath as I sucked on the head of his prick, my spit sinking through the cotton of the underwear to wet the bulbous tip.

Damian's body was rigid, stone-like, and I could tell he was fighting against his growing arousal, but when he must have realised there was no point in fighting this, he gave in. A soft sigh passed his lips and he stroked my long hair, gathering up handfuls of it but not pulling, just letting it flow like blond water through his fingers.

"That's beautiful," Jockey said. "My boys loving each other they way they're meant to."

The material of Damian's underwear was soon drenched with my saliva as I sucked and tongued the swelling warmth underneath it. At last a purplish knob poked above the waist band, the jockey shorts no longer able to contain it. A glistening pearl of pre-come seeped from its slit. I pulled it gently into my mouth, my tongue slipping down the shaft under the cotton, feeling every pulsing vein, savouring the sweet salt must of the man.

While I sucked my *brother's* cock, Jockey wandered off to fetch a tape measure and his own copy of Damian's contract. He returned and sat down opposite me, Damian's mostly-nude and exposed body forming a depraved line between us.

"That's enough brotherly love for now," Jockey said. "Mike, I want you to go sit by the couch. It's time for Damian to remove his underwear so I can take his measurements."

Damian, still calm and composed, raised his ass up and slid the briefs down. When they reached his knees, Jockey took over taking them off for him, sliding them down over Damian's hairy legs and big feet before pressing the underwear to his face.

Damian smiled at the sight of his new master taking a whiff of his gruts. "How do I smell to you?"

Jockey gave the question some consideration, the briefs another sniff, then said, "Like a faggot."

"I s'pose that makes sense," Damian replied, unperturbed. "After all, that's what I am now, right?"

"That's right." Jockey's response was muffled by the underwear as he took another big inhale of Damian's ball sweat.

I envied Damian's ability to remain so composed. This was undoubtedly a fucked-up situation, and one I'm sure he didn't want to be in, but Damian rocked a lazy smile and acted like this was all totally normal.

My former babysitter even remained composed when Jockey dropped the underwear and pulled his phone out to begin taking pictures. Starting at Damian's bare feet, and slowly working his way up to Damian's blinking face, Jockey made sure he photographed every detail of the naked man's front half—even making Damian lift his arms so he could take shots of the black hair in his armpits.

"Roll over so I can do the other side," Jockey said.

Once again the length of Damian's body was caught on camera, including zoomed-in shots of his asshole after Jockey made him spread his cheeks. Every now and then Jockey would stop to write something down in the contract, no doubt describing what he was seeing, before taking more shots of Damian's body.

"You can turn back over now," Jockey said when he was done.

With a heavy breath, Damian rolled over so that he was flat on his back, genitals on display. He'd softened somewhat since I'd sucked his dick, the most obvious sign that he wasn't enjoying the inspection. He stared up at Jockey as if to ask *what do I do now?*

Ignoring the questioning look on Damian's face, Jockey sat on the floor and grabbed Damian's balls, jostled them in his palm, then wrote something down in the contract again. My assumption was it would have been along the lines of *reasonable-sized balls and hairy* since that's what they were.

Nudging Damian's semi-erect cock with his index finger, Jockey told him, "Get it hard."

Damian grabbed hold of his dick and began tugging, closing his eyes while he pictured whatever fantasy necessary to deliver an erection. It felt like ages before there was any sign of life in Damian's dick, but Jockey didn't complain.

"I'm hard," Damian eventually whispered, eyes still closed, and released his cock.

Jockey admired the modest brown prick for a moment before lining a ruler against it and writing down its measurement into his copy of the contract. I didn't have to wonder what he'd written down because he told Damian.

"Your dick is five and a half inches long," Jockey said. "Not six and a half like you claim."

"Are you sure?" Damian sounded surprised.

"Rulers don't lie, Damian." Jockey glanced down at him like a stern headmaster. "Only little-dicked faggots do."

Once again, Damian took it all in his stride. "Sorry, boss. At least now I know."

After telling Damian that I too had "lied" about the size of my cock, Damin was lectured on the importance of accepting he had a small dick.

The Damian of a few days ago would have said something, maybe even threatened violence, but not this Damian; the one who had just signed a contract giving another man ownership of his ass. Maybe it was his experience through whoring, or maybe just because he was older, but my former babysitter didn't put up a protest and simply nodded before delivering the chant that was expected of him: "My name is Damian Takarangi and I have a small penis. My name is Damian Takarangi and I have a small penis. My name is Damian Takarangi and I have a small penis."

This pissed me off on Damian's behalf. The guy wasn't small. Modest, yes, but not small. And neither was I, damn it.

The rest of Damian's inspection required him to be on his feet. Jockey measured his height, his shoe size, waist, chest, checked his gums and teeth. By this point Damian only had one last body part that needed to be inspected...

"I want you to go bend over the couch," Jockey said. "It's time to see how loose this cunt of yours really is."

Damian chuckled, completely unoffended, and made his way to the couch. "I ain't loose, boss. I've kept by backdoor nice and tight."

"I guess we're about to find out."

"I'm actually looking forward to it," Damian said, wiggling his ass like a cat on heat. "It's been ages since I've had a decent bumming. And I'm keen to find out how big you are."

Damian wiggled his ass again, all faggy like, while Jockey stood behind him and rolled his eyes.

When I glanced at Damian's face which Jockey couldn't see, it suddenly dawned on me just how untruthful Damian was being. His actions didn't match the steely gaze in his brown eyes; a look that screamed murderous thoughts.

So it is all an act! I felt like I'd just uncovered a scandal. *But why is he pretending?* This was especially confusing to me because when they'd sat down and gone over the contract together, Jockey had told Damian he preferred his faggots to tell him the truth rather than tell him what they might think he wanted to hear.

Draped over one end of the couch, Damian waited for the inevitable fuck he was pretending to want so badly. I too was waiting, eager to see if my former babysitter could feign enjoyment while Jockey fucked the shit out of him.

Taking his sweet time, Jockey came and stood behind Damian's upturned ass, just staring at it.

Damian clutched his ass cheeks, spreading them open so Jockey could see the hole. "I'm ready when you are, boss." When Jockey didn't respond, Damian cheekily added, "Chuck it in, bro."

"Hold your horses, bitch," Jockey said. "I need Mike to get you wet first."

"Get him wet how?" I asked naively.

"Lick him out," Jockey said with some urgency. "Your brother needs to be juiced up for the fuck."

"But... but I've never done that before."

"It ain't rocket science, bitch. Spread his cheeks and lick."

I slowly made my way over to Damian and his exposed anus. Thick black hair gathered in his crack, surrounding a tight-lipped hole. It looked moist and loaded with flavours that scared me. I dreaded to think how many days it had been since his last shower; Damian wasn't renowned for his hygiene.

A week ago I had wanted desperately to stick my cock inside this man who I had known since I was a child, mark him as the first man I ever penetrated, but right now all I could think about was that this hole was where his shit came out of.

I couldn't do it. There was no way I could stick my tongue in his—

"Do it," Jockey barked. "Or you can piss off home."

I huffed out an expletive and leaned in, giving Damian's ass a cautious and hesitant lick, tasting salty-sweet skin. I was about to reel back from the foul stench emanating from his asshole but Jockey pressed the back of my head and forced my face deeper into the swampy crack of Damian's ass. "Get that tongue in there," he said. "I want you to make sure that dirty shitter is squeaky clean for my cock."

I did as I was told, tonguing the tangle of wiry ass hair and drilling into Damian's soft, hairless sphincter. The sweat, as sour as it was, was fine. But the thought of what else was caked in those hairs turned my stomach. I closed my eyes, not wanting to see what I was licking. The smell was worse than the taste. It was like festering compost, a sickly-sweet stench that spoke of dark secrets.

Damian opened his legs further to give me better access. I heard him say, his voice gasping, "Yeah. Just like that. Lick my shithole, Mike."

The word shithole was not what I wanted to hear right now, but I suppose that's what it was and I was certainly licking it. Grabbing hold of his lightly-furred ass cheeks, I kept licking at him, circling his hot, slimy hole with my tongue. Its taste was intense—base and filthy—and yet I found my cock hardening in spite of myself.

Damian writhed about on my tongue, moaning softly as my tongue cleaned away his sweat. I closed my eyes, imagined it was Jockey bent over and panting beneath the wet flicks of my tongue. If any man had an ass worth munching it was Jockey. It seemed a total waste that such a sexy ass belonged to a strict top.

I don't know how long I feasted on Damian's ass, but I think it was about twenty minutes. Long enough for Jockey to finish a beer and two cigarettes while he stood back and watched. When Jockey finally gave the order for me to stop rimming, I pulled away, gasping for clean air.

"Good job, bitch." Jockey gave me a pat on the head. "That's got your brother nicely lubed."

Remaining on the floor, I scooted out of the way and watched as Jockey sank down behind Damian's upturned ass. He stroked a finger down the Māori man's spit-soaked crack then pushed two skinny fingers up Damian's shitter.

Damian hissed in shock, but didn't object.

A hungry, hurting sensation swept through my chest. All resentment at being made rim Damian's stinky ass was replaced by jealousy. I wanted it to be me bent over that couch. I wanted that slender finger wriggling inside my asshole. I wanted all that come that would be shooting out of Jockey's powerful cock.

"Are you fucking me with a condom?" Damian asked.

"What do you think?"

Damian let out one of those infectious Māori boy giggles. "Hehehehe. Guess not. It's more fun to fuck a bitch raw, am I right?"

"You're right."

"I don't usually tell fellas this but if I'm the one being shafted then I prefer it bare. If my ass is gonna get stretched then I want the cream as a reward." Another boyish giggle. "Hehehehe"

"I'll make sure to give you plenty of cream," Jockey said dryly.

"Just try and go slow to start with, bro. That's all I ask."

Jockey finger-fucked Damian the whole time they spoke, invading him deeper and deeper with each upward push.

Turning his face towards me, Jockey said, "Mike, go grab me the lube from the top drawer beside my bed."

If you had lube why did you make me rim his dirty ass? I kept the thought to myself and fetched the desired item.

"Okay," Jockey said, pulling his finger out. "I think it's time I add your pussy to my list of conquests."

Instead of undressing, Jockey simply unbuttoned his camo pants and lowered them enough to release his dick and balls. He drizzled the lube over his shaft, slicked it around, and wiped his hand clean on Damian's lower back. Then with a quick jerk, he gripped Damian's hips and hoisted him up so his ass rested on the arm of the couch. Jockey gave his cock a few slippery strokes, then slapped it against Damian's thigh. "Are you ready?"

Damian nodded.

Jockey bent his knees and placed his cock against Damian's lubed-up, stretched-out hole and he pushed.

"Oh fuck," Damian gasped. "That's bigger than I was exp—" The last word got lost to a drawn-out moan as Jockey fed Damian another two thick inches.

Fascinated, I watched my master's girthy prick slowly descend inside Damian's entrance. Jockey did not rush, went slow and easy, allowing Damian time to adjust to the invasion. Once he was fully embedded, Jockey waited for Damian's breathing to relax and, without warning, he ignited his rhythm.

It wasn't the masterful performance I had expected. Just a sharp, short fuck no longer than a wank. One minute Damian was white-knuckling the couch, gasping "fuck, fuck, fuck" and other mindless profanities, and the next Jockey was grunting as his sinewy frame shivered in orgasmic tremors.

"I can feel it," Damian whispered in awe-like wonder. "I can feel your seed, boss. Mmm. You're filling me up."

Jockey said nothing, just rode the last waves of his orgasm before slowly pulling out. A sticky string of cum connected the tip of his cock to the deposit he'd made in Damian's ass. He broke it off by wiping the sticky head on Damian's furry butt cheek, grunting dismissively.

"Fucking hell, honkey. How big is that thing?" Damian squawked as he glanced over his shoulder to get a look at the dick that had just seeded his asshole. "You're packing way more meat than I expected. No wonder I felt that."

"It ain't that big," Jockey muttered.

"It ain't that fucking small either." Damian wiped sweat from his brow. "It's gonna take some getting used to being fucked by that on the daily."

"I'm sure you'll be fine," Jockey said, putting his dick away.

While Jockey patted down his crotch, and Damian stroked his slowly-closing bunghole, I was left wondering what had happened to the brilliant fuck I'd been expecting to witness? If I couldn't experience the power of Jockey's dick for myself then I had at least wanted to watch another man brought toe-curling pleasure by my master's talented cock. But that's not what had happened. It was all so anti-climactic.

Jockey walked over to Damian's discarded clothes and picked up Damian's underwear.

"What you doing with those?" Damian asked.

"Putting them on the conquest pole," Jockey replied. He went and hung them up beside the pair of mine already dangling above his bed.

"They look good there," Damian said, sounding far too smarmy. "I guess I should feel honoured."

"Yeah, I guess you should," Jockey grumbled, not looking very happy for a man who'd just emptied his balls.

"Is it all good if I go use the toilet?" Damian asked. "I've got myself a bunch of white warriors trying to colonise my colon."

I laughed at Damian's rare show of wit. Jockey, though, just shook his head. "Not yet. I wanna add another load up there first. But you can put your clothes back on and help yourself to a beer from the fridge."

Jockey hadn't even finished his sentence before Damian was up and fetching his jeans. Slipping his long legs into the denim material, the freshly-fucked faggot made his way barefoot and shirtless over to the fridge.

"You bitches talk amongst yourselves. I've just got to go outside and make a phone call."

Grinning with a beer in his hand, Damian asked. "Top secret phone call, is it?"

"Something like that." Jockey finally smiled. "I've just got some business to take care of."

As I watched our master walk outside, I couldn't help but wonder what sort of business he had to attend to at this time of night. All I knew was it couldn't be anything good.

Chapter 21

THE MOMENT JOCKEY WAS gone, Damian's regular demeanour returned and his mood soured. Muttering something in Māori under his breath, he helped himself to one of Jockey's cigarettes to go with the beer he was drinking then sprawled out on the couch, his shirtless body taking up maximal space. He looked like a man relaxing after a hard day's work, not someone who'd just been fucked, bred and owned.

Keeping a safe distance in the armchair off to the side, I didn't speak at first. Partly because I could tell Damian didn't want to be spoken to, and partly because it felt like the moment needed respect. Regardless of how lacklustre the fuck had been it didn't change the fact that Damian and I were now linked forever. We had both accepted the seed of a greater man than ourselves. Whether or not Damian agreed with that didn't matter. The important thing was I believed it.

Jockey Savage was our superior.

I'm not sure when the exact moment was it all sank in so fully, but I now knew that moving forward I could no longer dismiss the hierarchy, or the rules that governed it. If Jockey wasn't an alpha male then how had he managed to convince two men—two very different men for that matter—sign their asses away for his personal use and ownership.

When the tense quiet finally got too much for me, I asked Damian, "Are you okay?"

He looked at me then, eyes shining in the dim golden light of the room, but he didn't say anything. Just sucked in a breath of nicotine and let the smoke slowly exhale like a cloud of gloom.

"Did you want to be left alone?" I don't know why I asked this. It wasn't like I had another place I could go unless I went and sat in the bathroom.

Damian spat in his hand and pinched the cigarette out. Dropping the butt onto the floor, he turned and looked at me, like he was mapping my face to find the best place to smash his fist.

"You and me need to get a few things sorted," he said, voice as menacing as the darkness in his eyes. "One: you don't tell anyone about me signing that contract or any of the sex shit that goes on. If I find out that you have then I promise you, Mike, it will be the last thing you ever do. Two: you only ever do stuff with me if Jockey orders you to. Don't think for a fucking second that just because he says we're brothers that it gives you the right to touch me. And three: after this year is up you will never, and I mean never, speak to me again."

I said nothing.

Damian's lip curled in a snarl. "I should have known your mate would pull a shifty on me. He's a devious little maggot. Just like both his brothers. And his pisshead uncle."

"But I thought you and Darren got on?"

"We did. But that doesn't mean I ever trusted him. The whole town knows what the Savage boys are like. They've got a reputation."

"Yours ain't exactly too shit hot either, Damian."

"I do what I have to do to get by," he snapped, sounding like he actually believed that lie. "Your mate Jockey is devious just for the sake of it. Most white cunts are. No offense."

"If you're so pissed off with him how come you've been acting all...nice and shit?"

"Because I ain't giving him what he wants."

"What does he want?"

"Don't pretend you don't know." Damian glared. "It's pretty obvious."

I gestured as if to say *spit it out already*.

"Your mate is a sadist. He gets off on hurting people."

"Jockey isn't into physical harm. He's said so himself. And he didn't exactly go rough on you before, and he could have very easily."

"Nar, but he likes to hurt people in other ways. Mentally, emotionally...psycho shit like that. Dude gets off on control."

"That's what you said about me the night I hired you."

"And I stand by it. But the difference between you and captain spastic is that he knows how to get what he wants...and get away with it. Thankfully you're too fucking clueless and don't know your dick from your elbow."

"Fuck you too!"

"I don't mean it as an insult. It's good you don't know how to be a sadistic asshole. The more a man goes down that path he can get himself into trouble. Trust me, I've done it myself in the past." Voice hushed, barely above a whisper, he added, "With some of the women I've dated."

"I still don't really know what you're talking about."

"You will do the longer you stay under that twisted cunt's rule. Guys like that can be dangerous, Mike, especially if you don't know how to handle yourself. Thankfully I do."

"You mean by pretending you love what he's doing?"

"Exactly. The more he thinks you're enjoying it the less he will be into it. Eventually he will grow tired of the games and just leave you alone until he finds a new toy he can try and break."

I wasn't sure if I agreed with everything Damian was saying. Jockey was all about loyalty, and that loyalty surely would lend itself to him remaining interested in us—his toys.

After fifteen minutes, Jockey still wasn't back, and I began to wonder where he'd gotten to. Just before I was about to go look for him, he came inside with a big smile on his face. "Good news, boys. We have ourselves a guest of honour who wants to come and play with us."

"A guest of honour? Aren't we lucky." Damian said with mock excitement. "Who is it, boss?"

Jockey pulled his phone out and started swiping and tapping at the screen. Before he flipped the phone around to show us, I heard a video playing of someone saying familiar words in a vaguely familiar voice.

"I'm loose by Moose. Loose by Moose. Loose by Moose."

When Jockey turned the screen around, I saw what I had expected: my former school colleague, Isaac Fraser, getting fucked by that skinhead dude who worked at the adult entertainment store in town.

While I blinked in shock, and Damian's eyebrows flew up like windowshades, Jockey smiled back at us like the crazy sadist Damian had said he was. "Moose says he can't wait to meet you both."

Jockey had always said that was his favourite of the Hickford Homo videos, but he had never once let on that he actually knew the guy. While I don't suppose he had lied about anything it still somehow felt dishonest.

"How do you know that guy?" I asked.

"He works at the shop I buy all my naughty toys from."

That makes sense, I thought. Considering how much kinky apparatus Jockey stored in his wardrobe it was no wonder they knew each other.

My throat tightened. "He's not coming here to—"

"Fuck you?" Jockey shook his head. "No."

"Thank fuck for that." I laughed nervously. "I watched that video at home and there is no way I could take a cock as big as his."

"That's why he's fucking my other faggot," Jockey said, smiling at Damian. "The one with a more experienced pussy."

"Hell no, bro!" Damian shook his head. "I'm not letting that skinhead cunt bone me. Moose has been trying to get into my pants for years. I never let him. No matter how much cash he's offered me."

"You know him too?" I asked, dumbfounded.

"Everyone who cruises Hickford Park knows who Moose Daniels is," Damian explained. "The dude is there all the time, always on the hunt for some dumb cocksucker he can bend over and rip to shreds. But like I said, I always tell him to back off. I ain't letting no skinhead piece of shit nut inside me."

"Former skinhead," Jockey said. "He isn't like that no more."

"I don't give a shit. He isn't fucking me. End of story. I have principles."

"It's a bit fucking late for your principles," Jockey said sharply. "You signed a contract and I owe Moose a favour."

218

"Then you bend over for him," Damian huffed.

"Fine," Jockey said. "Guess we better go straight to the police station then and show them the video of you breaking in."

Jockey's words acted like a gunshot going off to silence a crowd. The quiet was eerie, and felt dangerous.

"You've done this on purpose," Damian whispered sulkily. "Invited Moose around just to fuck with me."

"I invited him here to fuck you, not fuck with you."

"You know what I mean. You're trying to mess with my head."

"What makes you think that?" Just the way Jockey said that made it quite obvious Damian was right.

"You were pissy before that I didn't react the way you had expected. Didn't crumble at your feet like this silly bitch does." Damian pointed to me just in case I wasn't sure I was the silly bitch. "So you've gone and called your mate up who you think can get you the result you want. I ain't stupid, Jockey."

"I never said you were."

"Then admit it. Admit you called him just to break me down."

Taking his time to respond, Jockey said, "You're half right. It is to fuck with you. But I do actually owe the guy a favour. He's giving me a discount on some stuff at his shop in exchange for letting him have a crack at your pussy."

"That's fucked up," Damian muttered. "Even for a Savage."

Jockey dismissed the insult at his family name with a shrug. "What can I say? Sex toys aren't cheap."

"You can't fucking lend me out to some racist fuck just so you can buy yourself a dildo."

"Actually, it's a fuck machine. And yes I can. Your contract states very clearly how I have the right to lend you out provided no harm comes to you."

"How the fuck is no harm going to come to me?" Damian bellowed. "The man has a footlong cock!"

"Footlong cock." Jockey scoffed. "Moose is big but not *that* big."

"I don't know the guy's exact measurement but I've seen him fuck boys at the park. His dick is massive. There's a reason he makes them say 'Moose made me loose.'"

"Moose is very experienced and knows how to fuck without injuring his partners."

"I don't give a shit. It's not happening!" Damian folded his arms in a huff. "No siree."

"Look, Damian, if you have an issue with it then leave. The door is right there. No one's forcing you to stay. Otherwise shut the fuck up, grab yourself another beer, and wait for Moose to get here so he can cash in the favour."

Damian looked like he was about to explode. But he didn't make a move to leave. Instead, he walked over to the fridge and grabbed another beer.

Chapter 22

AN HOUR WENT BY AND there was still no sign of the infamous Moose Daniels. During that time though, Jockey had ordered Damian and I to get changed into our very own army outfits. We looked fucking ridiculous, dressed like we were about to crawl on our bellies along the jungle floor, but Jockey looked damn pleased by the sight of what he called "my sexy little soldiers." It turns out my army-obsessed master had the outfits in both our sizes, just hanging up in his wardrobe—the one he always kept locked. If he hadn't been expecting Moose to visit then I wouldn't have put it past our childish master to take us to a park with toy rifles and play war games.

Since their standoff earlier, Damian had polished off three more beers and shared a joint with Jockey. It had pacified my former babysitter enough for him to keep his mouth shut but I could tell beneath his stoic exterior was a storm of anger and resentment brewing—not at all helped by being forced to dress up like he was bound for a tour of duty.

"It's been over an hour," Damian said. "I don't think your mate is coming."

"He's coming," Jockey said. "Moose never lets me down."

"There's a first time for everything," Damian grumbled.

"Don't worry, soldier. I'm sure Sergeant Moose will be here soon."

"I'm not worried. I don't want to see the racist cunt. I just want to go home so I can shit out your cum." Damian raised up off the couch and tugged at the set of his pants. "I can feel it leaking."

Jockey smiled. "That's hot."

"It's really not," Damian whispered.

Right then there was a knock on the door, our couch and chair-sitting privileges were over and Jockey ordered us to sit on the floor by his bed. This was a custom I had become used to but I could tell by Damian's sneering face that he would take a while to accept his role as a floor-sitter.

Moose came in, dark and mysterious, dressed all in black from the long-sleeve shirt to the ripped-at-the-knees jeans, clunky leather shoes and a small black bag he carried with him. The man was every bit as busted as I remembered: tall, malnourished-looking, shaved head, crooked nose, cauliflower ears. Not pretty. Clearly he'd been quite the brute in his younger day, a frequent giver and recipient of violence. The stubble on his scalp—sprouting like five o'clock shadow—proved he wasn't bald and shaved his head by choice, which made me question Jockey's claim that Moose *used to be* a skinhead.

In person he was every bit as ominous as the man in the video who had wrecked Isaac Fraser's schoolboy asshole. I hadn't picked up on his dark energy so much when he'd served me at the sex shop, but tonight he was oozing sex and danger, playing the role of foreboding big-dicked villain.

Stood beside the couch, he openly rubbed his cock through his jeans, the outline showing just how much he carried behind the denim. It was substantially more than anyone else in the room.

After manoeuvring the weight of his dick into a more comfortable position, he sat down. His eyes landed on me, and they quickly swooped over to Damian, like a bee looking for a new flower to pollinate.

I tried to gauge how old he was. I'd picked him to be about thirty-five in the video but now having seen him twice in person I realised he was probably older. My best estimate was early forties, but it was hard to tell. His face was weathered from years of hard living but his gangly body had a rugged fitness about it that made him seem a little younger.

As Jockey fetched his guest a drink, I waited for an introduction that never came. Instead, Jockey joined the noodle-limbed man on the couch; the pair perched like birds of prey on a telephone wire. They would occasionally look in our direction, but they only talked to each other, acting as if Damian and I didn't even exist.

Damian sat beside me, rooted to the spot, only his eyes moving, darting in their sockets from Moose to Jockey and back, again and again, following their conversation with his eyes— those smoky, smouldering eyes filled with rage and frustration.

I too observed the alpha males. I studied their body language, listening to the tone of their voices—quietly taking notes in my head for any future book I wrote that needed a believable villain. I noticed that Moose's left eyebrow had a few wild hairs that sprouted out of place, and this gave one the impression that he had a crazy streak in him. That kept me entertained, allowing me to somehow hover above this bizarre scenario involving two faggots and the men who planned to fuck them.

My book character daydream crash-landed when I heard Moose's gravelly voice say, "Which one of your cute little soldiers has the tighter hole?"

"Mike's is tighter," Jockey replied. "But Damain's pussy is in a lot better nick than I expected it would be. I thought with all the whoring he does he'd have a bucket ass."

"He charges too much for that," Moose said knowingly. "The pretty young twinks at Hickford Park offer the same service for the same price so he's mostly just getting sucked off in the toilets for a tenner."

Jockey smirked. "That so?"

"Yeah. I've been going to that park for years so I've seen it all before. The circle of Hickford hustler life. They turn up as dumb teens thinking they can make an easy buck. Then they nearly always get hooked on something which makes them whore their asses longer than they ever intended. Eventually someone younger and prettier comes along and they find the work dries up. I'd say your faggot there would be lucky to get bummed once a week, if that."

"So what you're saying is I shouldn't expect him to bring me home much money?"

"No. Unless, of course, you diversify the services he offers."

"How would I do that?"

"I hold sex nights above the shop once a week and the men who come along are happy to pay good money for the right sort of entertainment. Its demanding work but the boys are well paid."

Something about this conversation felt rehearsed. Like Jockey had wanted Damian to hear this, wanted him to know what could be in store for him moving forward if he didn't cooperate.

Continuing with his spiel, Moose said, "Ever since that Hickford Homo scandal erupted I've offered a safe space for men too scared of being caught in the park with their pants down. I pocket a bit of cash for hosting and they get their rocks off knowing their face ain't gonna end up all over the internet. It's a win-win."

"That sounds like such a great service," said Jockey, who couldn't have sounded more like an infomercial guest if he had tried.

"Personally, I don't give a flying fuck if people know I'm rooting at Hickford Park. I'm just like, I love cock. Sue me. But there are plenty of men in this town, mostly married and in the closet, who don't want their reputations damaged. That's why I started The Factory."

The Factory. Why does that sound so familiar?

And then it hit me. The ad I had read on the Hickford Homo website. It was by Moose. He was the guy who managed The Factory.

Moose pointed his beer towards Damian. "I've been admiring that one at Hickford Park for years. But he likes to play hard to get. Did he tell you that?"

Jockey chuckled. "He mentioned it."

"I've been telling him he doesn't know what he's missing. Told him I could make him feel good. But he always tells me he ain't interested in being made loose by Moose. It's a fucking shame cause he's very much my type."

Jockey raised an eyebrow. "Really? So you are actually into him? You weren't talking shit about that over the phone?"

"Yeah. Of course. Why the surprise?"

"Well, it's just that I thought your tastes were a bit...paler?"

"Not always. I like me some brown meat on occasion. Especially ones like him who pretend they don't like cock and are only in it for the cash."

225

"*Him* has a name," Damian said.

Moose laughed. "I know your name sweetheart, but you're not part of this conversation so be a good girl and keep quiet."

"Fuck you, ya skinhead cunt."

Moose laughed and turned to Jockey. "He's a feisty fucker. You've certainly got your work cut out with that one."

"That's why I invited you over. I thought you'd be able to help fuck some respect into him."

Moose grinned broadly, one side of his face twitching with an excited tic. His eyes darted toward Damian, while mine landed on the slowly-growing crotch of Moose's black jeans. His big meat was bloating in anticipation of accepting Jockey's offer. I marvelled at the strength of those worn-looking denims, now that they had a real problem in cargo retention.

I wasn't the only one who noticed the man's growing arousal. Jockey too had seen it. "Christ," he said, "just how much dick are you packing in them jeans?"

"Quite a bit," Moose replied with a salacious wink. "If you're interested I'll give you a chance to find out after I've fed your faggot's pussy."

Jockey dismissed the offer with a laugh.

"You ain't fucking me," Damian said, apparently to himself since both men ignored him. "You hear me? I don't do skinheads."

"Seriously though, Jocks," Moose said, still pretending Damian hadn't piped up. "I could rock your socks off if you let me. How many times have you been to my store and heard me compliment that dreamy ass of yours? It's gotta be the sexiest ass in town."

That's something we can agree on, I thought.

Jockey laughed again. "Thanks for the offer, but I think it's best if you just stick to Damian's asshole for tonight."

"Well, it couldn't hurt if you wanted to learn. . . sort of broaden your horizons. A good fuck up the ass never hurt anybody."

"You talking from experience?"

Moose chuckled. "I forget how old school you are about this hierarchy stuff. It ain't the end of the world if you let a bloke poke your bunghole. And yes, I have been known to bite the pillow on occasion. It doesn't happen often but there are times when even I need a good dicking."

"I don't need one and never will," Jockey said flatly.

"Well, you be sure to let me know if you ever change your mind." Moose grinned, an insinuating, taunting expression, and I felt my cock lurch with excitement. The thought of watching Jockey take a cock up the ass would be like a wet dream come true.

Jockey shifted, like he was uncomfortable. It reminded me of how he'd been with Darren—awkward and fidgety. Clearly my master struggled keeping up his alpha facade around men more confident and experienced than himself. Rather than think any less of him, I found it endearing, and it made me realise that part of my role moving forward would be to install the confidence Jockey needed not to wilt around other alphas.

Shifting his focus to Damian, Moose said, "I know you and me have never really had the chance to properly talk at the park, but I just want you to know that I genuinely think you're a really sexy fucker. You know that?"

Damian blinked, uninterested.

"I mean it, Damian." Moose did know his name, and he spoke it with desire. "I don't normally pay for it, my dick's reputation means I get all the young hotties wanting it for free, but I've always shook money at you because of how badly I wanna do you."

Damian appeared to relax a little, greased up by the compliment. "Thanks."

"Beautiful men like you don't have to say thank you. Just let us mere mortals admire their beauty."

What the fuck? Moose was laying it on a bit thick, but it seemed to be having the desired effect on Damain who even started to smile. I'm sure the pot and beer had helped but clearly my former babysitter was a sucker for ego strokes.

Moose continued to play the role of a skinhead Casanova, using trashy charm and toilet humour like he thought they were an aphrodisiac. And although Damian slowly smiled more and more, even laughing at a couple of Moose's bad jokes, my former babysitter didn't look any more likely to give his ass willingly to Moa Hill's version of John Holmes.

That was until Moose opened the small black bag he'd brought with him and pulled out a glass pipe and a tiny plastic bag of...

I didn't know. But I knew it was illegal and I was pretty sure it wasn't potato flakes this time.

Damian's eyes lit up, hands running up and down his legs. When Moose asked him if he would like to smoke it with him, Damian's ass was over by the couch in a heartbeat.

Moose opened the small plastic bag and started scooping out lumps with some straw-like device and filling the small, heavily tarnished bulbed-glass pipe, which he then stuck in Damian's mouth and held a lighter to. As Damian sucked, the bulb filled with smoke like a miniature crystal ball.

"Fill it, boy!" Moose urged excitedly. "Fill the ball!"

As Damian did, Moose took his finger off a hole in the pipe's side, releasing the precious chemical on the final part of its journey from whatever foreign land it had come from.

"How do you feel?" Moose asked.

"Huht ... Huht ..." Damian raised a finger of acknowledgement as he fought to keep the smoke in. Then, finding a space on the sleepout floor, Damian pulled a twenty-five second handstand.

"Wow! Pretty good, I take it!" Moose mused aloud.

"Pretty fucking good!" Damian told him, and then had another blow.

You fucking idiot, I thought to myself. Quite obviously this was just a bribe to convince Damian to cooperate. But I suspect Damian knew that, yet he did it anyway.

Within minutes of the pipe being put away, Damian was stood barefoot and shirtless in front of Moose, willing to give the older man what he wanted. The only assurance Moose gave Damian was "Don't worry, baby, I'll put it in nice and slow."

Moose really wasn't an oil painting and I seriously questioned what was wrong with boys like Isaac Fraser to pursue a man with such munted features. Was being fucked by a humungous cock really that worth it?

"How about a kiss first?" Moose said to Damian.

"I'm not into kissing, bro. Sorry. I'd rather you just fuck me."

"Call me old-fashioned," Moose said as he tweaked one of Damian's nipples, "but when I'm about to fuck somebody I like to kiss a little first." He caught my eye as he said "fuck" with a cold intentionality that gave me a chill.

Without waiting for permission, Moose leaned forward and pressed his thin lips over Damian's mouth. Damian grunted, probably from the shock of the man's greedy tongue invading his mouth, but he didn't push Moose away.

The kiss went on and on with Moose's hands roaming up and down Damian's back, reeling him closer so they were pressed crotch to crotch. Meanwhile, Damian just stood limply with his arms at his side as he endured the sloppy kiss.

"Right," Moose said when their mouths parted. "Let's fuck."

With one hand groping Damian's crotch, and the other shoved down the rear of Damian's army pants, Moose slowly guided them to the centre of the room, turning side-on so both Jockey and I could get a good view at Damian's front and back. With deftly finger movements, Moose managed to undo Damian's pants with just one hand, sending them sliding all the way down to Damian's bare feet.

"Mmm. So that's your pretty brown cock," Moose said, looking down over Damian's shoulder.

"Yeah." Damian gasped as Moose wrapped his gnarled fingers around his soft prick.

Moose kept his other hand on Damian's ass, rubbing slowly up and down, and I noticed he was keeping his middle finger in the cleft between Damian's cheeks. Damian gasped when Moose suddenly pressed deeper into his ass crack, finding the recently fucked anus with his middle finger. "Damn boy, what's got your pussy so nice and wet?"

Damian's mouth opened and closed like a fish trying to breathe out of water. "That's, uh, from Jockey. His...you know...his load."

"How kind of him to get things all ready for me."

Moose let go of Damian and began to undress, revealing a heavily tattooed body, smoother than I had expected, and a cock blessed with so many inches its owner probably didn't need a partner to have it sucked. Beneath the man's big ugly cock rested two massive balls, each one bigger than both of mine put together.

He made Damian step forward, out of his army pants, so that they were both fully naked. "Down on your knees, sweetheart."

Moose's voice was husky with rising feeling, and his eyes were narrowed to slits, watching intently as Damian moved—slowly, to be sure—in obedience to his order.

Crouching, then kneeling, going down on all fours, Damian's body radiated vulnerability. Moose followed him, squatting behind him, one hand on Damian's hips, the other hand riding up and down the widespread cleavage between Damian's tensed buns.

"I've waited a long time to get inside this ass of yours." For emphasis, Moose gave Damian's buttocks a ringing slap, and then cupped one cheek in firm, clenching fingers. I could see Damian tense in resistance and expected an outburst, but he bit back any bitter words he might have wanted to cry out.

Damian's head dropped forward onto the floor between his arms, patiently waiting to be fucked by a cock that gave my own ass phantom pains.

Moose stroked Damian, his whole back, his sides, and slowly worked his hands around to the front, fingering Damian's nipples, pinching them until Damian's head arched up from the floor. Moose laughed softly.

"Fuck, baby," the older man said. "I'm gonna fuck you good. Better'n you ever had before."

"As long as you're quick about it," Damian said, lowering his face back to the floor. "I don't want that honky stick in me too long."

"I'll do my best."

"Good. Then maybe you can let me have another go on your pipe?"

"That can be arranged... right after you've smoked this one." Just in case Damian didn't get the crude Joke, Moose slapped his cock against Damian's ass cheeks.

231

I stared in awe as Moose fed his cock into Damian's cum-filled asshole; slowly, gently, cautiously, obviously having learned from past experience that if he wanted his partner to last through the performance he had to take it easy.

As Moose continued to press forward, his cock must have hit a barrier inside Damian, and this time it was painful. Damian hunched his back up to try and pull away from the invader.

"Why are you running from the dick, boy?" Moose clutched Damian's hips and pulled him back. "Just open up and let me in."

"Ah! Unh! It's hitting something in there. Wait! Wait! Ahh! I don't think it's gonna....ooh!...go in any more."

Rather than pull out, Moose simply bent his knees slightly to shift the angle of entry, and thrust forward. With the more upward angle, Moose's big cock pushed right past the inner barrier and slid all the way inside Damian, right to the base. Moose held his cock firmly in Damian's rectum and kept his hands locked on his hips.

"Ooohhhh!" Damian moaned.

Moose's body pressed close against Damian's, his belly pressed firm and possessive against the furry, brown curve of Damian's ass cheeks. "That's it, baby" the older man said. "Well done. You're a very good boy."

"Holy shit," Jockey muttered under his breath.

Holy Shit indeed, I thought. The ruthless skinhead had just rammed his whole giant prick, to the balls, up into Damian's asshole.

My former babysitter winced and writhed, and then slumped, limp, passively taking it all the way in his rectum. I couldn't tell whether it was merely helpless acceptance of the inevitable or whether he had melted in passion at the sheer awesomeness of what his ass had swallowed to the hilt, seemingly without too much effort or pain.

"I can't believe you got all that dick in him so easily," Jockey said, sounding more than a little excited.

"Who said it was easy," Damian grumbled into the carpet. "It feels like I'm giving birth backwards."

Moose gave Damian's back a soothing rub. "Don't worry, baby. Now the real fun is about to start."

Then Moose fucked him. And I mean, really fucked him!

Having rearranged Damian's insides to accommodate his fearsome cock, Moose began to long stroke Damian with abandon, sliding balls deep on every in-stroke, and yanking his whole cock out of him on every out-stroke.

"Fuck, fuck, bro," Damian said. "That dick...fuck."

"Yeah?" Moose chuckled. "You like my dick, baby?"

"Big. So big." Damian's eyes rolled back. "T-Too big."

Moose grabbed hold of one of Damian's legs, positioning him like a dog taking a piss. Damian became a grunting, babbling idiot as the cruel new angle allowed Moose to thrust deeper and much more savagely.

Soon, Damian was panting as if he really were in labour, his furled fingers white-knuckling on the carpet. "You fucker," he snarled. "Just fucking come already, bro."

"In a minute."

That minute turned into five and the room became filled with the raunchy odours of their fucking. Moose was literally fucking the shit out of him. Each time his cock returned from its long journey in, coming out into the open air, it was more obvious that he was dragging all kinds of crud out of Damian with it. As foul as it was, I was mesmerised by this most brutal of fucks.

The older man pounded in and out of Damian, fucking him thoroughly, deeply, totally, the way a well-endowed man would have fucked a woman whose opening had long been stretched to receive such a colossal organ. The engorged shaft filled Damian, drove its way deep inside him. It was something not to be stopped, no matter how deeply it went, no matter how unready for it Damian was. It was making its own path, ripping aside all that was in its way, invincible.

I don't know if it was pleasure, pain or the drugs, but Damian looked out of it. His head thrashed about, teeth biting at the air, while he made noises that sounded more animal than human.

Not content to watch from the sidelines, Jockey left the couch and went and sat on the floor right in front of Damian's bobbing head. While I'm sure our master wanted to get a closer look, it also felt like he was purely sat there just to rub his new faggot's face in the submission he was enduring.

"I think somebody is enjoying your cock more than he thought he would," Jockey said, pointing between Damian's legs.

He was right. Damian was hard, and not just hard, he was leaking spunk all over the carpet.

Damian, barely with it by this stage, attempted in vain to explain. "Nar, nar...it's the button. He's pushing a button...I-I can't explain it but he's..."

"Cunting you," Jockey said, his wordsvoice icy and cruel.

Damian's eyebrows flung up, and he suddenly looked lucid again, a real look of fear crossed his face. "N-No! I didn't agree to that shit." He tried to scramble forward but Moose skewered him back onto his cock.

"It's too late," Jockey said smugly. "It's time for you to be the bitch you were born to be."

Damian shook his head, moaning. Then, like a dying man uttering his last words, he choked out, "I'm so glad I got to watch Darren get ass-raped in prison."

Moose was too focused on fucking to hear what Damian had said, but I heard it, and so didhad Jockey who sat there like he'd just been slapped across the face.

"You fucking what?" Jockey stared into Damian's dark eyes, demanding an answer. "What did you say, bitch?"

But Damian was gone again, his eyes rolling back as he moaned about how big Moose's cock was. Jockey, who still resembled a stunned mullet, came and sat beside me. He didn't say anything, just watched the brutal buggery in front of us as Damian's moans grew in volume and Moose's cock gathered more dirty ass juice.

"Fuck, fuck, fuck," Damian grunted deliriously. "Your dick...so big...so much dick."

"Don't fight it, baby," Moose said. "Just take the dick and say the words. You know what ones. You've heard the boys at the park say them."

Damian's head bobbed in a nod and he began to say what I imagined was a well-repeated phrase at Hickford Park, "*I'm loose by Moose, loose by Moose, loose by Moose.*" Over and over. "*Loose by Moose, loose by Moose, loose by Moose.*"

If I wasn't so turned on I would have felt sorry for him. I'm sure one of the few things Damian would have still prided himself on was having never said those demeaning words. But now he had. And he couldn't unsay them any more than he could get Moose's cock to unfuck his asshole.

I began to think the ageing skinhead was going to drill Damian's ass to the point of rectal prolapse. You couldn't take a cock that big, that hard, without doing some sort of damage. Yet, despite his ass being torn to shreds, Damian's cock seemed to have a hot, horny mind of its own—stiff and leaking, it didn't give a shit whether his ass lived or died.

And then it happened. Something I had never witnessed, or imagined happening.

Damian's manly grunts became girlish howls of bitch-lust as he collapsed on the floor, his body spasming like he was having a seizure. His body wouldn't stop trembling and a milky, watery fluid poured from the head of his cock. I assumed he was ejaculating. But then that milky, watery substance started gushing, and it turned a faint yellow. The dirty fucker was pissing himself! Pissing urine and cum! It came out of him like a fire hose, soaking the manky carpet so badly that I could smell the mingled flavour of both fluids.

"*That*," Jockey whispered to me, "is what cunting looks like."

Moose wordlessly continued pounding Damian's hole, picking up the pace as his climax approached. Beneath him Damian clung helplessly to the floor as Moose jackhammered his asshole. The room was filled with the slurping, squishing sounds of their coupling. Moose tightened his grip on Damian's hips, face scowling. "Gonna shoot... ah fuck...here it comes..."

With that, Moose let out a grunt, like someone at the gym deadlifting a massive weight. He drove his engorged cock fully up inside Damian and held it there as his balls flooded Damian's spasming body with his pent-up load. He slowed his thudding hips, and rubbed Damian's shaking back while he finished emptying his semen up Damian's ass. Finally, Moose eased his shit-flecked prick out of Damian's cummy opening and got to his feet.

I watched in awe as Damian lay crumpled on the ground, shivering in a puddle of his own piss, quietly chanting through chattering teeth, "*L-loose by Moose, loose by M-Moose, l-loose by*

Moose." Eventually though the words got lost to a new round of orgasmic bitch-moans and his dick let loose another wave of cummy piss.

Moose stepped away, sniggering. "My bad. I didn't expect it to be so fucking easy to cunt the bitch. Suggests he was never much of a man in the first place." The older man looked down at Damian with derision. "But that don't surprise me. His kind never are."

I couldn't be sure what the rude bastard meant by that but I had a fair idea, and I didn't like it. As much as I wanted to say something, call him out, I didn't dare. Not because of Jockey but because I was genuinely worried the lanky prick would pin me down and do the same to me that he'd just done to Damian.

Moose staggered over to where we were sitting. "You'd be best to put the bitch in chastity for the next few days. Make sure the cunting takes hold."

"Does that help?" Jockey asked.

"It's not absolutely necessary but it's the kindest thing to do. Helps their asshole get accustomed to its new role as a cunt."

"Okay."

"He's gonna be spaced out for a while so keep a close eye on him. When he stops shaking just put him to bed and give him a fuck first thing in the morning. You'll notice the difference. He'll be much more receptive."

"Thanks, Moose. You're the man."

While Jockey and Moose continued to discuss what they called *the new Damian,* I couldn't take my eyes off my former babysitter. He'd fallen from grace in my eyes years ago when he'd got hooked on drugs and turned to a life of petty crime. But this, whatever the fuck this was, was a far greater change than anything he'd endured prior. I could tell by the foggy look in his eyes that this was a changed man, and I'm sure I could see a tiny part of him crying out for help, like he wanted someone to rescue him from the overdose of pleasure coursing through his body.

But instinctively I knew there was nothing I could do. Nothing anybody could do.

Damian Takarangi had been cunted.

Chapter 23

IT WAS SO LATE BY THE time I left Jockey's place that the birds had started chirping. On the horizon I could see the slither of sunlight sucking my hometown towards a new day. A day that would see the official start to my contract. Jockey said he would text me when he woke up and give instructions about where to meet him. He'd said he wanted to take me some place nice, treat me a little, welcome me to my new life as an owned faggot in style.

As I walked past the local shops on my way home, my excitement about Jockey and our date was marred by what I'd just walked away from at Jockey's sleepout— a broken Damian. I couldn't stop thinking about what I had witnessed. The corrosion of a grown man. Jockey had said that if the cunting took hold, which he believed it would, then Damian would be a very different kind of person the next time I saw him.

When I had pressed for more information, all Jockey had said was, "Wait and see for yourself."

Well, I would be waiting a while because tomorrow Moose was coming back to collect Damian for 'pussy training school'. I wasn't surprised by that stage to learn that's who Damian's host would be, but I feared for my former babysitter's asshole if it spent a week being pummelled by that man's monster cock.

Before leaving, Jockey had made me clean up the mess Damian had made. I had wanted to object but it wasn't like Damian was in any state to clean up the mess he'd made. An hour after Moose had left, Damian was still shaking mildly, not really talking, other than occasionally muttering those sinister words "*Loose by Moose.*"

Shaking images of a naked, trembling Damian out of my mind, I walked up the driveway towards the front door, stopping at the doorstep to fish out my housekey. I dropped the damn thing twice before finally jamming it in the keyhole and letting myself inside. Creeping in the dark, I made my way down the hallway to my bedroom and closed the door. I didn't bother switching the light on. All I was interested in was going to bed and sleeping. I was fucking shattered. It had been a long day and night, and by the sounds of it I would need a good sleep so I had lots of energy for a big day ahead.

After kicking off my shoes, I didn't bother getting undressed, and fell onto my bed with a hearty sigh. But when I rolled over my face smooshed up against a rumpled piece of paper. I switched on my bedside lamp to see what it was.

It was a note from Gavin.

Mike,
Thanks for doing the dishes for me buddy. Look under your pillow for a token of my appreciation lol
Gavin

I lifted the pillow and found a pair of faded red briefs. *Gavin's underwear!*

Lifting them gently like a rare and revered artifact, I inspected every inch of the dingy red cotton, turning it slowly in my hands. There was the faintest stain in front and an even fainter whiff of the smell of its origin. I imagined piss dribbling from Gavin's cock, soaking into his underwear as he tucked it away, and my own cock rose to attention. I held the briefs to my nose and inhaled deeply. The heady aroma of dick sweat and ball musk made me shudder with pleasure, and I remembered how he'd said he had been wearing the same pair for three days now.

They smelled like it.

But they also smelled beautiful like the man himself.

I began to wonder if Gavin had left these here as a joke. Or did he know exactly what I would be doing with his pongy undies? I wasn't sure what was worse.

But I also knew I couldn't waste time worrying about it.

Led by my hard-on, and some very questionable desires, I got up to strip out of my clothes and lay naked on the bed. As I smothered my face with my stepfather's private scent, I thought to myself:

It looks like I won't be getting much sleep after all.

About the Author

ZANE LIVES IN NEW ZEALAND in a rundown pink shack near the beach with his gaming-obsessed flatmate and a demanding cat. He is a fan of ghost stories, road trips, and nights out that usually lead to his head hanging in a bucket the next morning.

He enjoys creating characters who have flaws, crazy thoughts and a tendency to make bad decisions. His stories are steamy, unpredictable and tend to explore the darker edge of desire.

Milton Keynes UK
Ingram Content Group UK Ltd.
UKHW040706201123
432908UK00001B/127